POSTTRAUMATIC

By

RONALD SIMONAR

EVENTHOR

TO ANNA

TABLE OF CONTENTS

PROLOGUE
WASHINGTON

THE SCREAMERS ARE at it again. Never was there a more unnerving opera. The steel bars offer no shelter to the choir members. At times the jarring quality of wailing voices ebbs to a single raw larynx but the effort invariably surges. Outside the walls, on a boarded-up street in a rundown part of the capital there is no hint of life within the Anacostia Asylum for the Criminally Insane. This is a private performance.

Eight miles to the west, the pinkish White House greets the spring morning flushed with the color of blood; the first blush of dawn. In the District of Columbia, it is the early hour. Timeless monuments glitter cold and electric. Whisks of clouds run up to the south. The morning is turning warm and humid with the occasional drizzle.

Take a look through the bars at a male patient. Being insane, one can accept that this man may have a reason to scream. You see him unclench his bloodshot eyes as pearls of sweat gather in old scars. You see him draw a breath, deep as his straitjacket allows and launch upon a full-throated bellow. It is a song so triumphant that it drowns out all the other voices that encroach on his private space. One more timbre to the great score. This is troubling. One scream is within reason, a concert is not. Maybe it is part of some healing program to get rid of blocked aggression? Perhaps they reward the inmates with food or benefits to share in this wild opus? As always there is a reason. As often, it eludes us.

This early morning, the lights are on in the bowels of the Anacostia Asylum. The Institute has a modern operating theater on the top floor but the auxiliary unit in the basement comes in handy mostly for the odd Postmortem. At this early hour, the basement dissection table is fitted with leather straps to hold down a bulky old man. His white and sallow skin, streaked with fresh seams of blood would raise an inquiring eyebrow in any postmortem suit. The fresh blood forms thin intricate patterns as it dries under the brilliant clique lights.

The crying old man is in obvious shock and clearly untouched by the clear radio voice of Donna Elvira. The morning opera carries softly from the background to blend into the more distant aria being performed by the disagreeing screamers on the upper floors. A heavy industrial machine by the wall is challenging both recitals with its empty growl; a Soviet-made combination bone-crusher and meat-grinder. This is an ancient type used in the Soviet Gulags to turn bones and slaughterhouse produce into the gritty essence of halfway edible soup. Converted from diesel to electricity, this antique grinder growls under a steel-framed Soviet poster from before the Second World War. The poster depicts a young blonde muscular man who raises his scythe above a field of golden corn. Behind him, on her knees, knowing her place, a woman gathers golden straws to her bosom. The two workers are cheered on by the idle multitudes of the proletariat, an unintended pun that is more prescient than the artist intended. Below this idyll, another bold prescient message is proclaimed in Cyrillic text.

YOU FOR ME AND I FOR YOU.

A heartbeat across town, the elected officials in the House or Congress use a more modern variation of the prehistoric proverb. 'You scratch my back, and I will scratch yours'.

No law passed on the Hill has ever failed to find harmony in that generous principle.

Another old man in green surgeon's scrubs attends the dissection table, even he of medium height and stocky built. The gray well-groomed hair is cropped short above a balding forehead that glistens in the warmth from the brilliant clique lights. Given the mood set by upstairs screamers, there is something vaguely sinister about this man, especially given the prewar Soviet poster. His bearing brings to mind the hulking figures on the Lenin mausoleum in long bygone days. The man speaks Russian.

"Too much bad vodka, Orlov," in a deep voice without humor.

For a moment, he studies the yellow-spotted fat-lined liver, weighs it in his latex-gloved hand, and chucks it indifferently into the grinder. The abrasive growl of the grinder softens slightly, and below the steel-framed poster, a mound of minced meat squirts into a steel drum lined with clear plastic. Above the drum, a single drop of dark livery juice lands to run down the poster glass.

A thick hand poses a small gleaming scalpel over an old, calloused foot. The old man waits patiently, seeking the left eye of his old comrade, the one still left in place. There is much to talk about. Later, after the old man's screams have wilted with his foot removed, the metallic sound of the heavy grinder turns briefly to a more labored tune.

The Anacostia Asylum for the Criminally Insane is owned and managed by an overseas fund with its seat in Luxembourg. Little is known of the anonymous owners except that their lobbyists on the Hill have deep pockets. In this capital, as every other, political survival is never measured in smiles.

The Anacostia Asylum is housed in a massive three-story cube of rendered concrete. The grounds in this rundown area near Fort Stanton Park are small and well-kept. Cast in concrete a decade ago, without a single window, its bulk feels like a fortress. Visitors, who enter this bunker, pass up the front steps through a small expanse of thick glass that is seamlessly sunk into the concrete. The glass gives a pleasant green hue to the marble reception. After dark, lit from within, the reception becomes a brilliant display of golden green. One would assume it makes a tempting target for the drive-by shooters in Anacostia who work unstintingly to make their mark on the neighborhood.

Some years back, there were times when the bulletproof glass reminded the few and furtive stragglers that passed the building more of a lunar landscape than the entrance to a medical institution. The replacement costs of the asylum entrance were inhibitive. Such attacks were rarer these days and the perpetrators were never repeat offenders. Should you take the time to ask, you would find that any repeat offenders had met with some gruesome fate or another; an outcome that raises few eyebrows in Anacostia. With two murders a day, nobody on Capitol Hill felt the need to ask why. In this part of Anacostia, the perps were all young and black.

On the desolate streets of this neglected part of the capital, expansive blank walls like these are known to arouse a prehistoric itch. Since time immemorial, man has portrayed the hunt on cave walls to raise spirits and mark territory.

Even today, many modern shamans in the slums are overcome with the urge to use the paint canister. This is the heartland of graffiti.

The walls of the Anacostia Asylum are spotlessly clean.

CHAPTER 1

AT A WALKING distance beyond Georgetown, in upper northwest Washington, lies the affluent residential suburb of Tenleytown, wedged between Glover Park and the urban sprawl of Friendship Heights. For decades, this inner suburb had been a sanctuary for political animals; one of the rare species unthreatened by extinction.

The houses are large and well suited for small fund-raising dinners of thirty-some; people willing to shell out a few thousand dollars for quality time with a political heavyweight. The plight of the inner city has made no inroads in this neighborhood. Weighed against the squalor of bankrupt Anacostia, Tenleytown is the Paradise where low profile political wives will forever continue to fine tune their search for chic restaurants and ritzy stores. And swap nonpartisan gossip, if nothing more exiting.

Framed by leafy acres, upstairs in a roomy bedroom of an elegant, timbered house, a gorgeous woman is lost in a large bed as she cuddles in sleep against a five-year-old daughter. The two are watched over by a dead husband; a dark-haired man in an ornate silver frame that is perched on a stack of books. The books are on medical research. All is silent. A framed certificate on the wall; Doctor of Medicine.

A clock radio flips a number, and the sweet voice of Donna Anna rises to engage the two in a seductive operatic passage from

Don Giovanni. The mother, entangled in her daughter's hair, is tickled in her dream by the whiskers of a large rat. This is not in the least disturbing to Dr. Caroline Glyn. At thirty-two, the former Mrs. Griffith is an authority on malignant cells. As the driving force behind the most interesting research project at the moment; carving up hairy creatures in the hunt for cancer-causing genes is routine.

In her dream, the first rays of sun strike through a jungle of laboratory glassware. The big rat raises its head inside the wire cage. The heartbeat of her child turns into drops that fall with a hollow sound from a leaky faucet into a laboratory sink. Lining the sink, stainless utensils await the rat's dissection.

This particular rat is too clever by half.

Caroline reaches into the wire cage where the curled-up rodent awaits its fate. The pink rat rises on hind legs to sniff the air, stretching upwards, rising to her hand. As she grips its muscular middle, the rat changes into a male reproductive organ. Caroline is holding a fat pink cock with whiskers. It feels alive, moving in her grip, wonderful to the touch. Caroline clings to this dream.

The man in the silver frame smiles.

In the odd hours of morning where fact and fiction mingle, Dr. Caroline Glyn is deeply enjoying her sleep when the alarm clock sounds. She wakes to stretch contentedly every which way under the covers while her dream slips away. After a relaxing shower, she works contentedly in front of the bedroom mirror to chase away the puffy remains of sleep. This daily ritual to preserve a beauty that would soon be deserting left a residue of guilt, but the weakness was strong, and she rarely abstained. It went against her deeply held beliefs to spend time on pointless labors like this; Time was a precious possession. Dr. Caroline Glyn puts aside a lipstick and admires her handiwork – still there. The fine wrinkles that spread away from her eyes were now as invisible as fine whiskers. She smiled at the thought, watching the marks of age. She smiled too much.

It was time to wake Mary.

Another measure of the uniqueness this morning was that her thoughts at the moment were not occupied with her research but rather with the Washington Post, which she found disturbing. Normally her first waking thoughts were on her work. She had become completely at ease with a life lived entirely through her profession. She loved every moment of it. The Washington Post article was due out today. Having come to believe that she hated the spotlight, she found it troubling how she had pulled all the stops to help the Post reporters to gather whatever material they considered relevant. A childish ambition to play the public hero was not a wise move, and about as upsetting as the daily exercise to hold on to fading beauty. The rewards in both cases would be fleeting. While taking care of her looks did rarely occupy her thoughts, the inner turmoil that came from public rites of self-glorification through the press was another matter.

Out on the porch, she picked up the morning paper and inhaled the humid air, heavy with spring. The neighborhood did not stir. She hoped the article had stayed on target; that Robert Noyes, the Post reporter, would leave out her comments on her social life, such as it was, and put the focus back on her work. She had mistaken his caring interest in her private life for kindness. Little wonder that a reporter seasoned in the interest of a broader public wanted more than the daily grind of medical research.

A biased story in the Post would doubtless make her name a topic at a reception or two. It would be a first after the death of her husband. Robert had been hugely popular with his valuable inside knowledge of official Washington, and since he passed away, she had not been to a single party. It would be a lie to say she did not miss being there on his arm. A lone woman who did not bother with politics in this capital, and cared even less about the latest Redskins game, was nobody's nominee for a table companion, gorgeous or not. In this two-subject city, malignant cells were not the most suitable topic for a dinner discussion.

The article proved to be an uncomfortable public intrusion into her private life, almost an out-of-body-experience. She felt like a boiler room rat, running an obstacle course through a scalding text that gushed on about her social life. Not once did the reporter note that her social life was a thing of the past. Her private likes and dislikes were sorted out one after the other and all of it cloaked the importance of her research. In some quarters, it would doubtless be considered an entertaining piece.

While Caroline made coffee, her daughter fended in her corner of the elegant breakfast table. The cereals ended more or less on her plate and some among the exclusive tableware. Sleepily, Mary watched Mom sort through the bulky morning paper. Weighing the alternatives, it seemed a good time to disturb. It was not unusual for her mom to forget to set breakfast altogether. Mary was fond of their dining room. It was a favorite place that struck the same solid tone as had her father, or so Mom had told her. Having inherited her father's raven-black hair, the child posed a stark contrast to her mom's pure gold.

"Can I have the milk, please," she asked politely.

"Of course, milk is good for your bones."

Caroline sipped her coffee with a grimace. When nothing else happened, Mary made a face at Babushka, a large rag doll propped up on one of the eight high-backed chairs. Babushka was smiling. Like her father in the bedroom photo, Babushka was always smiling. Annoyed by her mother's preoccupation, Mary started to read the front-page headline.

'Russia awash in weapons grade uranium!'

Puzzled, she shook her black curls and slid her thin frame off the chair. This was not English.

"Look, a picture of Mom," Caroline exclaimed on the other side of Russia. Mary came over to have a look, holding the milk jug. There was a photo of Mom with Alice, her lab assistant. Dr. Alice Christian had visited several times, but mostly she called Mom a lot on the phone. Unimpressed, Mary poured milk into her mother's coffee and returned to her seat. Caroline took another sip, this time without the grimace.

Mary studied her mother with wonder She never bothered with the morning paper. Today she was really focusing as she moved a hand angrily to a flushed forehead to brush away strands of hair. Must have something to do with her work.

"Bill will be pissed." For a moment she lowered the paper to stare blankly at Mary.

"Pissed off! Who is Bill?"

"Our Project Director, and a young woman must never use words like that."

Mary noted a new incredulous facial expression as Mom tried to hide behind the newspaper. The child did not know that this was the classic look of contradiction, rapt in both pride and shame. Mystified, Mary could not have guessed that her mother wanted nothing more at this moment but to vanish from the face of the Earth. She flinched physically away from the unwanted spotlight, as if caught in flagrante, bumping against the breakfast table, rattling the tableware.

"Shit"!

Mary made a surprised face at the equally dark-haired Babushka. She was about to point out that a woman does not use words like that, when her mom brightened.

"Listen, about your dad!" Her scholarly voice carried the deep measure of love that they both held for the man.

"When the renowned Dr. Robert Kingsley Griffith after a brilliant career in medicine, died of a mysterious brain tumor last year, he passed the torch to his companion and wife, Dr. Caroline Glyn-Griffith." Caroline slipped in a few words of her own, "to care for their five-year-old daughter Mary." She smiled brightly across the table. "Six months after his tragic death, his wife has fulfilled her vow to bring their common research into cancer-causing genes to a successful completion. Scientists are closely watching her latest breakthrough."

Caroline met daughter's eyes, and the child saw irritation behind the tears she attempted to blink away.

"Must they make everything melodramatic? And why is your breakfast all over the table?"

Mary ignored the angry question as another feigned routine, watching her sink back into the morning paper in a blend of misery and elation.

The telephone on the side table purred softly. It was a Federal inlaid cherry-wood sideboard with a serpentine top, valued at over twenty thousand dollars. It had been in Robert's family for generations. With her mother unresponsive, Mary slid from her chair to take the call.

"Hi Alice! Yes, reading the paper."

Mary handed over a cordless phone, reluctantly accepted.

"I cannot believe it. The whole article is off topic. This is all about my private life. Bill is not mentioned. How do you think I feel? Makes me feel cheap."

"Makes me feel great," said Dr. Alice Christian. A rare sentiment from a serious woman. She seldom sympathized with men in general and least of all with Dr. William Tailor, the nominal head of their team. She thought the man ashes all through.

"We need him to tap the money networks. He sold the Washington Post on this stupid interview, and he is not mentioned."

"Caroline, you are not his promoter. The man is nothing but trouble at the lab. He cannot leave the girls alone."

"So, he's a social animal."

"Animal, yes, not a bird with a broken wing."

"All his contacts will read this garbage." Caroline watched Mary grapple with a coloring book.

"Hurry up, dearest," she said halfheartedly, eat your cereals," then back to plead some more on the phone.

"I thought Robert Noyes was serious reporter. He told me the Post needed the background. I told him a few stories. Not for publishing, for spice. He promised me. This is a disaster, that dad had no education. It reads like a politician peddling himself, a crooked politician. It's embarrassing. Please remind me to be more assertive."

"Oh, my erotic instincts forbid!"

"What?"

"I do little else, my everlasting suckling."

"If Bill comes crying to you, remind him; it was his idea."

"We are not on speaking terms."

Caroline covered her eyes and squeezed her forehead to keep this trivia out of her thoughts.

"Check with our receptionists if any envelopes that came with my private bank statements have been filed."

"Your bank statements?"

"I need to know how they were posted. My bank manager called me to refuse my loan application. I had to tell him I never applied for one; not a quarter million or any other sum. Somebody hacked into their mainframe to change my address. Not easy with their security. Says they rerouted my statements to a dead-end post-office box. I always receive them unopened in the mail, as far as I know."

"You are kidding me?"

"My bank manager thinks it has been going on for months."

"Good God."

"Don't worry. Bank checked my credit and said no to the loan. What kind of con man tries to apply for unsecured loan in my name? I am not credit worthy after mortgaging the house to the hilt to help the lab".

"Did they catch him?"

"The bank asked the FBI to look into it. They haven't a clue, but no harm done."

"This is your life, Caroline. Talk to the police."

Caroline studied her laptop screen. "There is a new article on our altered genetic sequence on the Walter Reed database, published in France yesterday." Slowly her hand came down with the phone, placing it carefully on the table. After a focusing on her notes for a while, it became clear to Mary that mom was back to normal again. The child walked over, picked up the phone, said bye to Alice, and hung up.

Immediately, the phone started to purr again. Caroline jumped up and started to stuff documents in varying forms of disarray into a leather attaché case. She steered Mary towards the front hall. They heard a woman editor of a New York magazine make a pitch to the machine for an interview, promising loads of publicity for the cause. This was natural, the Post article read like an announcement for office. The media was going to haunt her for days, least while the public was buying.

"We got to scramble, where's your coat?"

"Don't want to leave Babushka."

"Babushka?"

"My new friend Krupskaya is called Babushka."

"Ah, you named her after your new friend. She's a fine doll. Promise never to accept gifts like that from your friends in kindergarten. And why this dance every time we leave? Kindergarten does not allow private toys."

"Why?"

"Think about it. What if the other kids cannot afford beautiful toys?"

"Babushka is a rag doll. And they all say they have rich dads."

"And what do you say?"

"I think we are poor."

"Hey, we may not be rich, but we are not poor."

"You told me we have no money!"

"Ah, that was just a minor cash-flow problem." Caroline smiled at Mary's questioning face.

There was another purr from the cherry-wood sideboard and the machine received an offer for her appearance on some midmorning chat show. Would Dr. Glyn-Griffith like to comment on the present state of stem cell research? The day was turning into a nightmare.

"Remember, if the world wants a song and dance routine, a woman must say no." She steered Mary towards the front door. "Why not ask Babushka to look after our home while we are gone? A good friend would do that!"

The child looked between her, and the smiling Babushka perched up on the dining room chair. For the umpteenth time, her mother realized she had a battle to win. Smiling joyfully, Caroline Glyn, formerly Mrs. Griffith, fell to her knees to embrace Mary's tiny waist in a game they often played, by now almost a daily routine. She cuddled her daughter, reciting an old ditty, gleefully tickling her ribs for effect.

"We are two of a kind, alone against the world. Let's make a pact; you for me and I for you."

Little Mary Griffith squealed in delight. The doll in the high-backed chair was laughing too. The gleam in her glass eye mirrored the homely setting as would any other hidden high-quality lens. Babushka did not mind watching their home.

As tortured reflections off a glass eye, mother and child disappeared out of a deformed doorway into a brilliantly lit spring morning.

CHAPTER 2

S HE BACKED HER old Saab-convertible down the driveway, only to hit the brakes as a superbly waxed Lexus blocked her path. It was Phillip Lehman flagging her down, which was funny at best. Her neighbor had barely exchanged a word since Robert died. She knew it stood to reason, a woman who had lost both her parents in a car crash three months before she lost a husband in cancer was unlikely to brighten anybody's day. Caroline was disgusted by how easily she accepted her own dilemma.

"Hi there Mary, you've grown," Phillip told the belted down child. "Good to see you, Caroline."

"Thanks, and how are you, Phil?"

"Holding up," he grinned, "it's been a while. How do you do that? You are more beautiful than ever!" This was his standard fare for the female gender. Phillip who was casually but carefully dressed would not be accepting any cynical replies.

"We are having a small dinner party tonight. Eugenia is always talking about asking you over. Never got around to it. The old gang misses you, so how about it?"

"Thanks, Phil, I'd love to come, but I have a lot on my plate."

"Tonight, if you can make it," and Phil was off with half the foliage of Tenley excitedly trailing his gleaming Lexus. She knew he had read the Washington Post. His words indicated he was aware that she would not be bringing a companion. When it came to such important details, her neighbors were watchful. Ready to challenge the rush-hour traffic, Caroline eased off downtown in a Saab convertible that suddenly seemed remarkably untidy. Vaguely irritated, she thought it would be great if Phil had commented on her work for once, instead of her appearance.

Robert had selected the Georgetown kindergarten because of its imposing record. Caroline suspected his choice had more to do with the background of its clientele than the quality of its education. Her late husband, breast-fed on references, found the values of Old Washingtonian circles important. It was the rear-guard action of old families trying to defend a fading social status on watered down finances. The grapevine suggested that this Georgetown kindergarten was up to standard for an only child. Its location demanded a time-consuming detour on way to work but lost time and hefty expenses had to be set aside. That it was Robert's decision, made her reluctant to cancel Mary's enrollment.

Kindergarten was an old converted private mansion in a lush part of Georgetown. The two-story brownstone, built on gently rising grounds, hid behind a high wall of golden red bricks that went splendidly with the black wrought iron gate. In the large garden, cherry trees were in full bloom. Pink blossoms lay thick on the paved walkway that curved from the handsomely pillared portico down to the gate.

Cars were barred from the grounds, and she parked in the spotless oak lined street, taking special care to find the right spot. The oversized oaks tended to block Mary's door despite determined efforts to open. On passing, Caroline glanced at the large brass plaque by the gate. Framed by a swirl of green Ivy, and polished to cheer up the dullest of mornings, God knew she smiled at it often enough. Outside the gate, a tall beefcake loitered by a stretched limousine and offered a cheerless smile that Caroline ignored. She walked her child up to the house with unassertive elegance, already in a better mood, the Post article all but forgotten.

On the flower-strewn path in front of them, walked a stocky old man with cropped graying hair, leading a child by the hand. Mary tugged at her and suppressed a mock giggle at the clumsy way the old man clamped his large fist awkwardly around the kids arm, high above the wrist. His powerful grip forced the child to walk lop-sided. Caroline responded to Mary with a firm shake of her head and pressed lips, but the do-not-make-fun-of-grown-ups routine did not fool Mary. Mom was having her own private chuckle.

Abruptly, the child on the path up front turned her jet-black head of hair. The beautiful face momentarily stunned Caroline. She stared in utter disbelief. A freak wind rustled the kid's black hair and died down. It was Mary's new friend, Babushka. It could have been Mary. The two girls were shockingly alike. Two peas in a pod.

The old man heard them and halted. Little Babushka hung like a rag doll in his grip. The old unsmiling face reminded Caroline of her late father and a mounting surprise made her cordial towards this luckless stranger and his lovely daughter. The man blocking her path must be the grandfather, she thought gracelessly, as she appreciated the anonymity of every detail of clothing. Gray suit under a gray coat and a gray nondescript tie worn with a vaguely striped shirt. If his outfit were a statement, it might be saying; do not notice me. His gray well-groomed sideburns framed a studious lack of expression. She could not read him; a man of strong character, she decided.

The old man released his awkward grip and they stood watching the two girls run up the path, picking blossoms as they went. Caroline offered a warm smile, looking for a trace of response in his blank eyes. There was none. It did not fool her; the gray eyes must be working hard to prevent the kindness escape. She felt sorry for a lonely old man, reduced to a baby-sitter for his grandchild.

"I am Rykov," a controlled, deeply resonant voice, "Krupskaya's father."

Poor Babushka thought Caroline, without meaning to.

"Aleksei Ivanovich Rykov."

On this introduction there sailed the moldy leftover of a Russian accent, so she made her introduction, impatient to get on.

"It has been brought to my attention that our two daughters have become good friends," the old man continued.

"They are so alike," Caroline replied, thinking the opposite. Thinking that in nature, two identical charges repel each other, thinking Mary, Mary, quite contrary. The old man spoke in clear well sentences; perhaps too clear and too well modulated. A sense of something contrived struck her about this meeting, but she could not get over the shock of the uncanny likeness of the girls. Was he feeling the same surprise? Was it therefore he plucked up the courage to approach her?

"I am pleased that they are friends," the old man added, as if granting a stamp of approval. Caroline ambled up the path, trying to shift her focus to the hectic day ahead.

"It is good to have friends," she replied distantly, again thinking the opposite. She never had time for friends, which was probably why she did not have any.

"An article in the Washington Post this morning has been brought to my attention, about your medical work. I will read it."

Another solemn declaration, another favor granted.

"I like for our two daughters, Krupskaya and Mary, to become better friends. Your daughter is of good stock."

A burst of mirth exploded in her. He sounded like a farmer discussing livestock. Robert would have liked his approach. If Rykov's message was in many ways common, it revealed a solid weight of authority that she was fond of. Beneath the granite surface, she guessed as much, lay the soft innards of a lonely old man. And where was the mother? The poor thing must be four decades younger to be of childbearing age.

In the reception hall, two young attractive, ruthlessly efficient women came to greet them, all personal smiles, and slow movements. The carefully ironed old fashioned cotton dresses in faded colors covered them to below the calves. This would reassure their clientele, as did the airy hall with a high ceiling, and tall windows framed by carved panels, painted in beige egg tempera. It came out superbly on film. Carefully chosen, the photogenic women were untouchable embodiments of morality. Horny Senators waving off their kids in their company would appear wholesome. The establishment knew its clients.

As Caroline passed Mary into their care with a wave, the old man's hand come up halfway to copy hers. She enjoyed the crack in his granite front. Like her dad, the old man loved his kid, and he would hide it away until the day he died. Holding this thought in a sociable mood, once out of the portico, Caroline slipped an easygoing hand under his arm. Finding him curiously unwilling she insisted. The old man relented. It was funny and she knew it by heart. Together they walked slowly down the path among the Japanese cherry blossoms, towards the gate.

"I live in a neighborhood like this, Dr. Glyn-Griffith," said the old man, "people are older. There are no children. It is important that my daughter have well-adjusted friends. I would like her to be," he hesitated, "loved Doctor Glyn-Griffith." Caroline appreciated his difficulty in minting a word so foreign to his tongue,

"Call me Caroline."

"That is good, Caroline. Krupskaya's mother is dead. I have only Babushka now. Babushka has only me."

She was right. Like her dad, hiding away his love where it was no-good to anyone. It was important to reach out. Caroline smiled at her own intransigence. The thought struck her. She was a loner and she liked it. When did she last reach out? To this day, she blamed her reserve for not braking through her father's shield before it cracked on his deathbed. He had lived three days after a head-on collision instantly took her mother's life. A driver of an oncoming truck had suffered a heart attack, but in the end, he was the only survivor. That was fate for you. When her father regained consciousness, he had lost the will to live. He had left his daughter and granddaughter with Robert holding the reins. Old men were a breed apart. Stranded at advanced age with a young kid was tough, the old block of granite walking beside her was molten and mushy inside. She suspected he was papering over his doubts, alone against the world, afraid of getting burned.

Caroline was impulsive by nature and always ready to show other people the error of their ways. As she about for a way to get through to the old man, all she came up with was a childish doggerel; the game she played with Mary half an hour earlier.

And so it was that halfway down to the gate, Caroline stepped up to the startled old man and gave him the same warm hug and rapid cuddle. She abstained from tickling his stocky frame. That was for kids only.

"We're two of a kind," she jostled happily, "alone against the world. Let's make a pact. YOU FOR ME AND I FOR YOU." Little did she know how these innocent words shattered the man beyond the mask. The fearless touch of friendship paralyzed him. Caught off balance, he looked confused. A long forgotten deeply suppressed vision came to him of his own father's death. He was in the Kremlin, standing over the bodies of both his parents. Beria was speaking.

"Comrade Stalin, what about the boy?"

Where did this long-lost memory come from? For the first time as a grown man, Aleksei Rykov realized the part his great leader had in wiping out his family. In those days there were ways to make a child forget.

Stalin watched him.

"Look at this boy. He is hard." The great leader spoke. "You are a piece of steel. If you are half the man your father was, let's make a pact. We are two of a kind, alone against the world. I am your father now, Aleksei. You for me and I for you."

Stalin turned to Beria.

"See to the rest of his kin. I want them wiped off the face of the Earth. Let the People's Commissariat of Internal Affairs straighten out the boy. When he is spotless, bring him to me."

Rykov looked at Stalin through six-year-old eyes, without anger. This was the great leader of the greatest nation on Earth. Stalin reached out for him and Aleksei responded to his foreboding presence. But as he entered the embrace, the touch became that of Dr. Caroline Glyn. The picture in his mind shattered by the young woman's cheerful laughter.

Smiling, Caroline stepped away from the old man as he regained himself, pale as a sheet.

How had this young woman brought forth such a hidden memory? He felt a moment of gratitude. That too was a novel feeling. "Yes," he still did not smile. "You for me and I for you. Let that be our pact. Once family is always sacrosanct."

The old man gave his hand solemnly. There was nothing for Caroline but to take it. She accepted his gesture of mock gravity. The old man kept his humor dry and well hidden, and she was not on her best behavior. This was his way of pulling her leg. A mock handshake was better than a snub. Rykov did not let go her hand. She gave him another small hug. A loving hug had never hurt anybody. As she broke from him with flustered cheeks, the thought how curious it was that the old man had responded to her charade like a young boy.

"I want Babushka to have a good home," he said cryptically as they continued down the path.

Outside the wrought iron gate, a stretched black limousine waited in the street with its motor running and driver at the wheel. Two unobtrusive security escorts approached from the other side, scanning the street. One was a burly blonde with three breasts and a two-way radio. The third breast was under her arm. The other was the young beefcake who had offered Caroline a broken smile a few minutes earlier.

"Yours, Mr. Rykov?" It surely was her day to play the fool.

"Yes."

"Have they rearranged the administration," she said, being clever. With his Russian accent, that was not a choice. "You are too old to be a Rolling Stone, and too kind to deal in drugs. Diplomat, are you?"

"I am an old-fashioned business manager. There have been obscure threats leveled at us by a Middle East terror group. I fail to see what they can want with a multinational trading company."

"Rather safe than sorry?"

"That is my policy."

"Mmm, who'd have thought, a woman bodyguard."

"Women often notice the small details, the loose threads," he gave her an empty look. "I should not discuss my security."

"Oh, I did not mean to pry."

"Good-bye, Caroline. And remember our pact."

The stocky old man entered his limousine. His security detail took a last look around, all low-key and professional. Caroline walked over to her Saab. A long time ago, it was said to be the car of choice for the creative crowd. Now it seemed dustier by the day. She would ask someone at the lab to take it for a spin to the nearest car wash. She buckled up and grabbed the phone.

"I'm late, Alice, is Bill in yet?" She watched the heavy black sparkling limousine pull into the street ahead of her and float away.

"Sure, can't you hear the wailing?"

"On my way."

About to ease her car into the street, she hit the brakes for the second time this morning as another massive limousine, gray this time, and equally sparkling, sailed so close it almost sideswiped her car. The red-white-and-blue diplomatic license plates came to a full stop up ahead, blocking her path. Cursing out loud, fumbling with meshing gears, she willfully calmed herself, then backed up before pulling out, carefully this time.

Alice had misread her outburst.

"No Alice, not cursing Bill, just another joker with diplomatic immunity. His limo almost ripped my side out."

As most Washingtonians, Caroline hated the international diplomats with private rules of the road. She put away the phone.

As she passed the gray Cadillac limousine, she glanced in the rearview mirror. A man in a pinstripe suit stepped out from behind one of the broad oaks a few yards up the street. He had the distinguished mane of an old gray lion. An aid jumped out from the front seat to hold open the gleaming rear door.

The gray mane ducked into the gray limousine.

CHAPTER 3

THE LABORATORIES WERE tucked away cozily half a mile from the campus of the National Institutes of Health in Montgomery County, inside the Beltway in Bethesda, Maryland. Caroline loved its location off Wisconsin Avenue; the drive from Georgetown took only fifteen minutes with heavy traffic going downtown in the opposite direction, and for once there were no construction detours.

Housed in a drab building, the rented one-story setup came with a parking lot. It was a modest location, fenced off by plain greenery. Caroline thought it lovely. There were a few birches in good health, her favorite tree. The rent included the services of a part-time gardener who tended the bushes and roses that bordered the outdoor terrace. It had a canopy and was a popular meeting place during coffee breaks.

This morning, Dr. Alice Christian, a caring but never cheerful personality, greeted Caroline on the outside steps with a smile she was unable to suppress.

"Switchboard is swamped. Interest's picking up."

"Who's in charge?"

"Who else; God himself."

"I do not want to get caught up in this."

"Don't worry; God won't let you within a mile of a reporter."

"How is he taking it?"

Alice gave a roll of her almond eyes, "nothing a shrink couldn't cure."

"Any messages?"

"Bags, but not the kind you want. I hear the Washingtonian wants in on the story," Alice found it hard to hide the smirk, "that would be your neighborhood bible. Doctor Taylor's favorite."

Caroline whined, "celebrity chatter". The Washingtonian was the monthly trivia paper for the wealthy suburbs, crammed with DC tidbits. She could imagine how they would angle the story into what they chose to call human interest. This was no longer about science.

"The City Paper also called to promise us an excellent feature if you gave them a private interview; loads of calls for your time."

"Christ!"

They passed a reception desk where two young women busily worked the phones. The younger girl rolled her eyes at Alice who shook her head and smiled at Caroline, "My spies tell me the TV networks are feeling us up."

"I thought you said that was Doctor Taylor's privilege."

This time, Alice managed to cut off the smile. "By the way, my girls have no old envelopes from your bank, they never keep them. What kind of a hacker would do that?"

"Right now, I would not put it past the Washington Post."

"Have you got any clue how much it takes to hack a modern banking system?"

Caroline shook her head. It wouldn't take much effort to cultivate a lecherous middle-aged bank manager in a city full of people with access to share for services rendered. Any dazzling young woman could pick up an employee at a local bar and have him on the hook within hours, if the rewards were worth an unbelievable roll in the hay to keep him keen.

"I don't want to think about hackers." They stopped, looking at the doorplate of Dr. William Taylor. "I hate dealing with unreasonable people," she added.

"Stand up to him, please. Cancer is the only culture he aspires to." Alice sighed. "There are more interesting rats waiting in the lab. I'll prepare a cappuccino", shaking her head, she walked away. Caroline knew she was right. She never dealt with unreasonable people in the way they deserved.

Even in early spring, Dr. William Taylor sported a Florida tan. The sharply dressed career researcher was her senior by a decade and worthless in a lab. He probably hated the grind but loved to think of himself as a scientist. Hired as an administrator after Roberts's death, he had proved his worth in securing funds. In the present research climate, this was a precious skill and although their financial problems had eased, she knew that would be a temporary spell. The time to pass the hat again was just beyond the corner.

"I'm the head of the project and they don't mention my name?"

"Bill, you know this, the light stuff always floats to the top, like muck in water." Caroline knew that teamwork was important for the long-term survival of her lab. The project was all that mattered. She had hired Bill for his fund-raising prowess, tempting him with a title that meant nothing, but his ego was always getting in the way.

Flanked by his spotless desk, Dr. Taylor looked bitterly out through the window and studied the birches. The office walls served as a hanging gallery of friends. Special care was given to framing signed photos of him with Nobel laureates. The all-male snaps from society dinners did not have the feel of friendship, which was a jaded term in Washington anyway. They were trophies like the books on medical science that took up the leftover wall space, gilded leather spines in prominent places. The floor-to-ceiling hardwood bookcases that were fitted and paid for out of research funds had caused their first row.

"Bill, we both know that most folks are not the least interested in what we do. The Post has become part of the popular press; they dramatize. Their got what they wanted." She was about to add, 'you got what you deserved', but held back

"It will hurt us with the money networks."

A twenty-something entered the office to place a folder by the family photos on his desk. Bill's features turned amiable. The young woman was new to Caroline. Bill gave the newcomer a body massage with his most charismatic smile, and Caroline fought the surge of anger.

"Nonsense, Bill. You are a bagman, not a politician. Every time a member of your political action committee raises funds for us, you kick some back to their candidate of choice. Their only interest is petty cash to push the agenda. The men who bundle the money care nothing about what we do here." She turned her attention to the shapely young woman.

"You must be our new lab assistant. Caroline Griffith. Welcome to the team."

"Leila Keller, happy to be here." Sensitive to the charge in the air, the assistant retreated as quickly as protocol allowed.

"I wish you would not call me Bill in front of staff," he said bleakly, as if Caroline needed the aggravation. Fuming, she tried to hold firm.

"This was our new assistant?" There is a long list of better qualified applicants; both genders."

He stoked her fire by staying willfully mute.

"She's not the one I recommended."

"Leila's qualifications are fine with me." He used her first name with a breezy familiarity, aware it would get on her nerves.

"Bill, we don't want your reputation as a hands-on man taken out of context. There have been complaints. What does this new plaything know about medical research?"

"You are a fine one to bitch, throwing the rest of the team overboard to grab the credit. Even your lipstick lesbian got better billing."

"What are you talking about?"

"Your dyke, Doctor Alice Christian!"

"Why do you say these things?"

"I'm not the one saying them. The reporter who hung around here last week with follow up questions about your background was very familiar with her Sapphic sophistication. He wanted to know if you and Doctor Christian were sexually involved. Is that your thing?"

"Seriously? The Post is a distinguished newspaper. They would never ask such a thing. Who was this reporter?"

"James Wright, I think, Robert Noyes's assistant, or so he claimed. He had heard some rumors about your financial problems, a less interesting story. Who's to say this lesbian chic is bad. I'd swear on the Bible that you have not let a man near you since I came here, but we've all seen Alice eat you with her eyes. Does she stop there?"

"I have never – I'm shocked."

"Wasn't me who brought up the sex angle."

She was a rational person, and this was not a rational conversation. Caroline stormed out before he could claim victory. He had mastered the technique of pulling her emotional strings. Too often it kept her thoughts off work for hours. She slammed her files down on the laboratory table a trifle harder than was called for. That was the extent of her public outburst. Pulling on her white coat, grappling with buttons, she tried to tone down the aggravation.

"Damned megalomaniac, I've seen them soak up the wine at Le Lion d'Or, not a sober thought among the lot of them. I don't think Bill would hesitate to blow our grants on candlelit dinners and fancy restaurants if we gave him half a chance."

Alice put down her scalpel and removed her gloves.

"You've been to that French museum? It should be off-limits for anyone with your figure."

"Went there with Robert once. Never eaten so much in my life. The butter cream sauces were fabulous. Doctor Jeremy took me there after the funeral. He greeted everyone in the place. We need friends like that."

"That bank ruse worries me. Have you talked to the police?"

Alice stepped over to help her with the buttons. Gave her an understanding embrace. Under the circumstances, it felt different. Caroline took her hand and squeezed it gratefully.

"Bill went too far today. Called you a dyke."

It was supposed to be a bitter joke that turned sour when Alice diverted her eyes for an involuntary moment. Caroline went into a flurry of nervous gestures, unprepared for a sudden new realization. It had never occurred to her. How could she be so stupid?

"Christ, an old Russian gentleman told me this morning that women are the observant ones. And look at me."

"A man told you that. You should stand up to Bill." Her assistant withdrew her hand and shook her head with a bitter smile, then moved to a working table to remove the sting of her presence, "the little prick is hiding behind your ideas."

Caroline started to raise her hand to face it head on. Not knowing how, she brought it to her forehead instead, the old habit of running away from personal problems. Perhaps that was why she did not have any. That was something to be grateful for. In her mind, she affirmed that the project was what mattered. She looked over at Alice who had put her gloves on and started to slice open a rat with an expert move to pluck out the affected tissue. Searching for a way around this, Caroline lashed out at Dr. Taylor.

"He knew it would spoil my day, making stupid remarks. It keeps me from concentrating. Why does he do that?"

"He's a man," her friend said in a tired voice.

"What the hell does that mean?"

"It means that the sum on his paycheck is inversely proportional to his intellect." Caroline had to smile at that. There was logic in that, but still.

"I have nothing against men. Robert gave me the best years of my life. I cannot begin to tell you how I miss him."

"Robert was special. Most men are like Bill, bumming a ride to the top. And you always give in to him."

"Jesus, Alice, you should have told me."

"My sexual preferences are none of your business, Caroline." Alice hissed and stabbed the rat with a force that left the blade implanted in the worktop. She stormed out of the glassed-in laboratory, ignoring a sleek scalpel that vibrated in perfect tune with her rage.

"It's not contagious," she whimpered on passing Caroline.

The door had barely slammed shut when Caroline's hand closed around the vibrating scalpel. Even now, there was only one thing here that mattered; the integrity of her experiments came first.

Continuing with Alice's task, the hidden microphones under the table barely picked up her dejected mutter.

"This is not going to be my day."

CHAPTER 4

I T WAS LATE afternoon when Caroline headed back to kindergarten. With the car top folded, she drove down Wisconsin Avenue as a pleasant breeze combed her hair. The air quality declined with the elevation towards Georgetown, a premonition of a mottled summer of heat and humidity. The stop-and-go traffic allowed her to consult a clutter of notebooks on the passenger seat. Try as she might, her usual serenity of mind was absent. She looked around instead.

The expense-account crowd was out in force, packing the shops and restaurants. Suddenly she missed her spring evenings with Robert. During the intellectually dormant summer months, they'd do the town with all his remarkable friends. They'd hobnob in Hill bars and watch the give and take among the young collegiate interns living rough in the dorms and sublet townhouses of Georgetown. Not much had changed. The same throngs roamed the streets. Young blue-eyes mingled with sure-eyed pros.

A heady potion of power roused these hungry minds and motivated the barter of young bodies. She heard the same carefree laughter as they heard back then and found again the wild smells of open barbecues. The sobering thought startled her; the drifting kids of ten years past were the professionals of today. Caroline shuddered at the ruthless march of time.

So much was lost, like playing softball on the Mall. And then, out of the blue a passing shower swept across the neighborhood and drenched her in the car, putting her notes in peril. As she fumbled to put up the roof, the air-conditioning came on instead with a soft whir that was drowned in the screams and hoots from coffee shop students scattering for shelter.

This afternoon she hunched to hug Mary more than was her custom, against the photogenic panels of kindergarten. Rewarded in kind, the raven-headed Krupskaya joined in. The sweet child would not be getting much warmth from her old block of granite. Her father was a poor substitute for a loving mother. Caroline felt sorry for the kid and treated both girls to the width of her affection. When she rose from this emotional display, she found the old man watching. She shot him a warm smile, expecting none in return and he remained true to form. If he approved, he'd never admit it.

Caroline picked Mary's coat off the hanger, shook water drops from the wet cloth, pleased that the kids had been allowed to play outdoors. She smiled when Rykov took his daughter by the arm and lead her in that odd lop-sided fashion down the path. It was not her place to teach an old man how to lead his child.

The spring shower had cleaned the air and passed on. Behind the old man, Caroline hoisted Mary up to feel her warm presence and cuddle and love her a little extra. The old man moved slowly, and she couldn't help but to catch up.

"I have read about your work in the Washington Post."

"A silly little piece, wasn't it?"

"My company wants to put up funds to support your work."

"That is very generous of you, Mr. Rykov, and deeply appreciated. Does your board realize that there are very limited commercial applications here? And anyway, money is the least of my problems right now."

"Why is that?"

Caroline detected a trace of surprise in Rykov's well-groomed voice.

"My problems concern the scientific research, not funding, and I am working full throttle. I cannot redouble my efforts. Too much money means time-consuming administration, and the work already takes up all my time. Maybe, with the Post article, raising funds will be easier for a while," she reached out to tap a cherry tree, aware it was a strange habit for a scientist. It was her late dad's habit, knock on wood.

She treated Rykov to a warm smile for his offer. Was he offering her a bribe to soften his conscience? Was he ashamed of his own weakness of seeking a pact with her and Mary to give Babushka a better future?

"Caroline, I am serious about my support. You will have all the funds you need to finish your undertaking."

His serious voice brought her down to Earth. She stopped in the middle of the path and looked at him for a while in pregnant silence. "That frightens me," she hesitated, "when big business throws money at a scientist, he becomes a bureaucrat. Forgive me, why would an international trading company sink its hard-earned assets into noncommercial research?"

"Babushka's mother died of cancer."

"Oh, I'm sorry."

"I read that your husband came down with cancer. I understand that he did not leave you well provided for."

"Ah, but you didn't read that in the Washington Post."

"Washington is a village, my dear."

"That's true but don't believe everything you hear."

"That is one thing I am never accused of, my dear. There are benefits in long-term stability, even privately."

"Yes, the house is leveraged and becoming a burden, but I earn good money and we get by famously," she cuddled Mary again, "don't we?"

"When your luck runs dry, so will the funds that back your research."

"I guess that's the American way. I must deliver or move on. There is no shortage of researchers willing to use your funds for their own benefit. That position is spoken for."

The old man turned to face her on the path. He studied her intently.

"Your funds need never run dry, Caroline."

"I'm grateful for any support you can give us, Mr. Rykov. I would not dream of refusing any contribution to our research, but I cannot promise a positive outcome and there are no patents coming out of this."

"Caroline, we made a pact. This morning, I took the necessary steps to secure your future. I suggest you allow Babushka to spend some time in your care. That is compensation enough for me."

"What?"

"Growing up in your care will afford my Krupskaya an entry into the world that she will one day call her own."

Caroline stared at him dumbfounded. Whatever had she said to give the old man this absurd impression?

"There must be a misunderstanding." In the rush of silent surprise, Caroline held her tongue and gathered her thoughts. There would be no question of any such responsibility.

Old Rykov let Babushka go, and Caroline lowered Mary down onto the flower-strewn path. The girls slipped away to pick Japanese cherry blossoms as they ran ahead. For a moment, her thoughts wandered untamed as she watched them run towards the gate.

And exactly at that point that the stillness of the morning was broken by a dim rumble of a distant explosion. Immediately, Rykov startled her by barking out to his security people in Russian. The rough order went unheeded. The kids slipped through the gate.

Ignoring her, the old man started to run stiffly down the path, thick neck shaking. Caroline recalled her overprotective father and felt saddened by this unseemly display. Krupskaya had become the old man's problem instead of his happiness. Rykov reached the black iron gate that was held open by the broad tall beefcake that smiled at her earlier this morning.

Caroline sauntered down the path a few yards behind, shaking her head when two loud cracks from the street rattled her. The old man bolted through the gate and bulldozed his way past the blonde who tried to block his path. Somebody should tell him it was a car backfiring. Her diagnostic mind rejected this out of hand. The cracks were too close to issue from a muffler. And why would that security woman be trying to block his way? She too started to run.

It was a grim scene. The black limousine was parked a few yards up the road. In front of it, the driver lay crumpled on the ground in a most unnatural position. His cap had rolled to a stop on asphalt spotted with the damp of the bygone rain. The driver had fallen across Mary, pinning her small wriggling torso under his bulk, too heavy to move. An unfamiliar grimace of pain marked her daughter's face. Caroline made a mad dash towards her. In front of the limousine, old Rykov had reached Krupskaya who lay there hidden from view. Out of the corner of her eye, Caroline saw him lift what seemed a lifeless body. In his powerful arms, Babushka looked like a limp rag doll.

The eyes of Aleksei Ivanovich Rykov fixed on a man with a lion's mane behind the large oak by the curb. His jumpy running gaze moved to Caroline in full sprint towards him. Behind her he saw Boky put a gun to the blonde head of his plump partner, Galina. His tall security officer pulled the trigger, the sound canceled by a silencer. Galina fell like a spiked cow as her heavy body crumpled to the pavement.

The trap, baited by love, sprang shut. It was a good setup, Rykov thought in that split second, taking in the mindless race of young Caroline, mid between him and Boky. Nothing but a bullet would stop that girl. With Babushka in his arms, failing to drop her in time to avoid the bullets, he turned to catch the fatal firestorm that issued from behind the broad oak. A semiautomatic hail of large caliber bullets tore through Babushka into his chest.

Caroline threw her body upon the spotted asphalt to try and protect Mary. Her mind was blank to anything else in a world where everything was in slow motion without sound. First, she tried to pry Mary loose from under the dead driver. With one slender leg buckled over the curbstone, her daughter cried out in pain, and she eased off.

"He hurt my knee, Mummy."

Flat beside her on the asphalt, Caroline put a hand under the raven head and tried her best to shield her with her body. Her analytical mind concluded that Mary had at most stretched a knee or cracked her leg. They lay barely two feet short of the dying old man and his dead daughter. For a long moment, Caroline watched Rykov cling to life. The mask of a lifetime had cracked open. He looked at her in desperate panic, his weak voice grating.

"He killed my ...?"

Tears welled up in Caroline's eyes as she reached her free hand for Babushka's head, so like Mary's, her eyes open and unmoving. Caroline put her fingers carefully against a small throat. There was no pulse.

"Your daughter is dead."

She said it simply, pushing away the mental panic. There was no need to spare his feelings. His torn chest was evidence enough. Yet old Rykov refused to die, reaching a bloody hand in her direction, trying to speak.

"Our pact... remember.... Touch me!"

"What?" It was her father all over again.

"Touch me," he croaked with the wheezing of punctured lungs. There was real panic raging behind his eyes. The mask was gone. He had fallen against the polished chrome of the limousine bumper with his dead child crumpled between them. Unwilling to remove her hand from under Mary's head, Caroline, on her side, stretched her arm across a small puddle of clear water to reach out to him. A long ivory finger with a perfect nail advanced across the void to touch a thick bloodstained sausage of a finger.

It was a moment of grace spoiled by natural forces when a visible spark of static electricity passed between them. It stung Caroline finger and she could not help her reflexes. By instinct, she pulled her hand back sharply. The old man did not withdraw his. Death had tracked the Minotaur to the heart of his labyrinth.

Caroline glanced up at the male security man who stood watching them from the pavement. She assumed from his upright position that the immediate danger was over, and she shook her head to tell him his master was dead, then went back to comforting Mary. Never in her life had any truth been so brilliantly clear as it was at this moment.

All medical research in the world did not amount to a hill of beans. She drifted, eerily watching the blood seep out of the old man. It collected in a puddle that slowly circled the crushed cherry blossoms the girls had dropped on the asphalt.

In curious detachment, Caroline marveled at how beautifully the two colors mingled, dark heavy red against the fleeting pink of a Washington spring. Eternity passed before she heard the faint sounds of sirens in the distance.

CHAPTER 5

N O SERIOUS INJURY, said the emergency intern at Georgetown University Hospital, testing her patience. "I will have a nurse take her down for x-rays when there's an opening. We are overwhelmed as it is. I must ask you to wait here in the hallway."

The lean young man with the horse teeth carried himself with the confident airs of a young god but Caroline found his untrimmed beard unusual for an ambitious doctor.

"Great lecture you gave here at Georgetown on malignant cells," he plodded on.

"Who are all these people," she asked, rejecting his praise.

"There was a bomb at Union Station!"

"Oh, God."

"You picked the worst time ever for a Georgetown drive-by. We are on our knees here." The intern looked her over, approvingly. Maybe it was the way the Post used her title, so unusual in a staunchly male chauvinist city. Dr. Glyn-Griffith, they called her, a distinction from her late husband. Her birth name, Glyn, gave off the aura of Old Washington. Maybe it was how she carried her blood-smeared dress like a badge of good breeding. It became more than a filthy garment.

"It was not a drive-by shooting," said Caroline.

The young intern sighed. The emergency unit had to cope with scores of casualties from the bomb that gave the swanky suburban mall at Union Station a black eye and left a good deal of wounded. Walter Reed and Washington on 23rd had taken the first pick. Georgetown Hospital got the leftovers, and it came on top of the spills from a gang-clash on L Street, a routine fare; two injured pimps and a teenage girl who might have caused it. They had just lost the young woman. Four dead on arrival from a drive by shooting in Georgetown were icing on the cake. The dead had infinite patience. They never complained.

"No serious injury! I will have a nurse take her for x-rays." The young god from Culpeper sounded cheerful, running his hands over Mary's slender joint. It had started to swell but the sedative had taken hold and relaxed the child. The probing caused no pain. The knee would hold. You could see that he was more worried about the celebrated mother. One explosion a day was enough.

"Can't you try to speed it up," Caroline appealed.

The intern understood why the hospital founders felt more at ease with her breed at arm's length. Georgetown University was the oldest Jesuit school in the country, and few schools of thoughts were rifer with sexual politics than was religion. His problem was that Caroline belonged to a selected group that was likely to unbend with the elite in his field, and she commanded a flame that drew hospital administrators like moths. Her complaints would be heard upstairs. Nonetheless, he pegged the female professor as a reasonable sort and played his hand deftly, giving her that extra nudge.

"I'll do my best, Miss Glyn. As a doctor, you understand our problems."

Caroline hated how his words held her in place. Yes, even with her daughter in pain beside her, she would be reasonable. Her deep-rooted servility was degrading. One look at her ingratiating smile had told the young god the secret of her life, that here was a woman who had perfected the art of behaving sensibly. She would never back down on scientific facts, but just about anything else was worth folding on, for her peace of mind. The intern walked over to the admittance desk and took on a harried black nurse. Snippets of a heated exchange wafted her way.

"She got juice in this town."

"A woman in this male chauvinistic city?"

"Can't you smell the aura of Old Washington?"

"All I smell is sweat. She'll have to wait!"

Cursing her high heels, Caroline wheeled Mary's cot gingerly over to an empty spot against a sterile white wall. Settling to stew in anger, she stroked Mary's forehead, comforting a child she had just betrayed by being reasonable. She thought of Krupskaya as her tearful eyes wandered between neatly dressed professionals crowding the hallway. It eased her mind that they had also put these folks on hold. They might not expect the unhealthy deference granted a senator but few of them would be sidelined without reason. She thought this to justify her inaction and she knew it.

Not too many years ago she had suffered the trials of an emergency intern. She had forgotten the stress of emergency rooms, the small-town variety. With the roots of her memories recently torn up with the death of her parents, all that remained of hometown thoughts was the stifling heat. She no longer felt kinship with that sleepy tobacco port on the Potomac River. It was an unremarkable childhood. Her father taught mathematics to reluctant kids in high school, and her mother ran a small beauty salon. It was a chapter forever closed that dovetailed perfectly with her present predicament. Everybody was dead.

"I'm sorry about Babushka," she told Mary who was sedated, and half in shock, "it won't be long now."

The place was carnage. Morosely, she watched staff work feverishly behind loose partitions to assess cases and shuttle them on. A disorganized fleet of cots kept bumping into each other, eliciting groaning protests from wounded casualties. Others, in limbo, waited morosely on hard-backed chairs, holding on to bloody makeshift bandages. Caroline fingered Mary's injured knee firmly to evaluate the apparently minor damage.

"Was them damn niggers doing a drive-by, Professor."

The man who attached himself to Mary's cot was Patrick Miller, the DCPD detective who took her preliminary in what she considered a biased session. The lieutenant had continued to drop hints, airing his opinion of a drive-by. Now she resented the way he took hold of the railing of Mary's cot. His broad forearm sprouted a crinkled mat of fair hair that reached down from the short shirtsleeve to the back of broad fingers. This was not his place.

"You have my preliminary statement, officer."

"Yeah, but a drive-by is safe. Telling you for your own good. Random killing is no danger to anyone."

She avoided his eyes. Felt soiled by them. They were eyes that did not care. Once upon a time, Patrick Miller had been a handsome man with blonde hair, firm chin, and fine bone structure. The years had not been kind to this bachelor, now in his late forties. His rise within the ranks had faltered. The spotlight passed on. Too much booze and too many cheap women showed through the soggy skin of his eyes. Caroline wanted no intimacy with this bloated bruiser, and he leaned into her hostility as if he enjoyed the intense aversion.

"What is the matter with you all," she bristled, "a drive-by shooting requires a moving car. As I told you earlier, somebody was hiding behind an oak by the curb. The murderer was waiting for the old man with a heavy weapon. You cannot square that with a drive-by shooting."

"You got nothing to gain by getting involved," he said slowly, his Virginian twang carried on a breath that came dangerously close to being an assault weapon. "Reckon that's the gospel truth. Put a finger on them guys, they come after you." He seemed no longer to be promoting a drive-by.

A hospital orderly interrupted, reaping a string of curses as the cot he pushed rear-ended a wheelchair. The orderly took the abuse with the same aplomb as the body on his roller cot, covered by white linen from head to toe. He parked the cot by their side.

"Can you look after her while I prepare the paperwork for your signature," he gave the lieutenant a nod and hurried away. Caroline had missed the opportunity to ask Miller to explain his change of mind.

"This a witness to a gang clash on L Street. See what I'm saying?" Miller narrowed his watery eyes. "Dispute over turf, random killing and nobody cares."

He let go of Mary's cot and reached to flick the sheet way back. Caroline shuddered. Maybe it was Miller's gold watch more than the sight of the woman's face. A watch as vulgar as the man. The dead girl was young and well limbed, black, and beautiful. Her eyes that ignored the hairy arm of the law were no longer looking for the Promised Land.

"My old man did not talk much," Miller confided. "Reckon he told me one truth. Folks don't wanna die, but they sure want to Heaven."

The lieutenant placed a large hand across a small dark throat and turned the head. There was a small entry wound at the temple. "This black trash is a beauty, isn't she, still warm. Was them damned niggers settling scores, doing the world a favor."

"What a morbid thing to say."

"Reckon she saw something she shouldn't. Found out the hard way she got no protection. That's your problem right there, Professor. Don't let them Fibbies tell you different."

"Fibbies?"

"Them Federal boys," Miller replaced the sheet and shook his head sadly, amazed by the evil in the world. "You got nothing to put up if them guys come after you."

"What are you warning me against, lieutenant?"

"Shucks, lady, telling you for your own good. Don't quote me on that, you hear. Kid's your weak point. They'll go for the kid."

"I don't understand."

"Sure, you Old Washington stock. I bet the Iron Triangle got all the evidence to clear this up, if they willing, they sure as hell don't need you to tell them what happened."

The detective looked leisurely at two men standing on the steps of the second-floor staircase, scanning the overflow of wounded. He lowered his voice to a whisper and leaned in closer.

"My advice; let the pork barrel fraternity handle it. They always get their way. Bend every rule in the book, believe me; you don't want to stand in the middle. Keep calm and this will go away. No sense getting carved up for nothing."

His breath smelled like an open sewer. Gasping, she turned, eyeing the cause of his unwanted discretion. A well-proportioned white man with a badge clipped to his trench coat stared at her from a staircase down the hall. She took up the challenge and locked into his gaze. They were friendly eyes that held hers easily. Suddenly there was this incredible current riding between them, as both refused to yield. The creature broke the spell as he stepped off the stairs to vanish in the crowd. She had found him incredibly attractive, and this powerful new self-indulgent feeling troubled her. She was not her normal self.

"Special agent Carl Smith, of the FBI," he told her, coming up. With a mild shock, Caroline realized that he was below average size, not as tall as he had looked from the distance. Nevertheless, the attraction held.

"Doing drive-by shootings now, Carl?"

"Hi there, Miller, no, but I need to sit in on this one."

"Till you know how to drop it," Miller said meaningfully and winked at Caroline. "Mrs. Glyn-Griffith has cooperated fully. Thing is, for a professor, her memory is all over the place. Must be the shock."

Caroline gave a vaguely amused smile. Had she hurt his feelings, was the bruiser giving some back?

"Dr. Glyn-Griffith?"

The agent turned to face he, looking her over with receptive eyes, and she needed a fair amount of sympathy as it was, and a broad shoulder to cry on. She was taller but she was the one wearing the elevated shoes.

"Caroline," she offered with a broad smile, but if the Metro detective got the snub, he didn't give it away.

"Caroline, this is special agent William Parker Jr. Can we talk away from this racket? Would you see to it, agent Parker?" Smith addressed a black man who had moved in his wake. The image of a tug pulling an ocean liner came to Caroline who felt irrationally amused. She stood corrected. Her misconception that the FBI Academy had a minimum and maximum height for enrollment was obviously untrue. William Parker was a well-built giant of a man. Whoever decided to pair him with agent Carl Smith must have had a hidden agenda.

"Jesus," Miller exclaimed, willfully overreacting to the big man. He pushed his loathing further by fingering the tag on Parker's coat lapel. He scanned the small tag photo, giving the black giant a hostile southern grin.

"Could've sworn this was a thumbprint."

William Parker Jr. returned the smile. A wide crack opened in his boot-black face, revealing a perfect row of pearly white teeth.

"You'd love the negative, Sir."

Agent Smith sneered at what was happening above his head. Caroline put it down to being ignored. If they were partners, when perps engaged the pair in a brawl, they'd go for Parker as the whipping boy.

"Would you see to it, agent Parker," Smith repeated as Junior wrinkled his nose at the detective. That nose had taken plenty of punishment and Junior was ugly by any measure. Caroline imagined that Smith had told him so. He might even have tried to imagine how it felt to look in the mirror every morning and meet red-rimmed eyeballs in a bootblack face. He'd probably find it better than being of medium size and christened Smith. He had met her eyes and felt the current run between them. It touched them both. Up close, maybe he had seen her surprise.

A little later, an angry nurse ushered them into a tiny room in the adjoining hallway and curtly grabbed hold of Mary's cot. The child had fallen asleep, hidden by the covers. The nurse claimed she was taking her for x-rays. It would take time. The nurse had no idea how much time. Only staff was allowed, and no, she could not have a copy of the x-rays. Caroline found it all deeply upsetting.

The tiny cubicle was bare except for an examination table. The instruments were securely locked up in sturdy cabinets where the clientele couldn't lift them. The four of them piled into a cramped space without chairs and remained standing. She felt sweat in her armpits as she pushed past them to pick a plastic mug from above the small sink. Her hands trembled so violently that she almost dropped the cup. She hated the taste of tepid water, attempting to resist the stifling depression that washed over her.

"You alright?"

Smith's voice had a rich timber. It allowed her to shore up defenses against the relentless rush of unfounded apprehension. She could not find any logical reason for this sudden fear.

"Yes, thank you," she lied, grateful for his concern, unable to account for her inner turmoil. Levelheaded under pressure by instinct and training, her students used to call her the hyperborean scorpion behind her back, citing her cold unemotional reasoning and readiness to strike. She found all of it unwarranted.

"In your words; how did this happen?" Agent Smith took the lead.

She tried to marshal her thoughts. If only Smith had been a bit taller. An unknown nurse had taken her child. Was that woman doing her job or was there something else? Why was this so difficult?

"Where do you want me to begin?"

"You arrived from work to pick up your daughter."

"Yes. I ran into Mr. Rykov, the old gentleman. He came to pick up Krupskaya." The name that she could not pronounce earlier came out so fluently that she stopped and repeated it in wonder.

"Krupskaya," she said, then pushed on apologetically, "we called her Babushka."

"This was not his routine!"

"I would not know. Ask the kindergarten staff. I met him for the first time this morning. He brought Babushka and we exchanged a few words."

"Earlier this morning, huh? What you talk about?"

"Nothing much, he was pleased that Babushka and Mary had become good friends."

"Right, and this afternoon," she felt how rapidly the agent lost interest.

"Rykov read a silly article in the Washington Post, about my research. He offered a contribution to my research, a financial donation."

"Why would he do that?"

"His wife died of cancer."

"His wife", there was a surprised exchange of looks with his partner.

"And in the afternoon, where did this conversation take place?"

"Outside, the girls ran ahead."

"Then what?"

"I heard the shots. No, wait, first the explosion, distant."

"That would be Union Station. Perfect timing. How many shots?", running her through it without much interest. Over the sink there was a small metal mirror. She did not like her looks and closed her tired eyes against a strange and growing depression.

"Two shots, I believe, a car backfiring was my first thought, but they were too close together. When Rykov, the old man, started to tun towards the gate, I followed."

"Go on."

"I saw Mary under the dead driver. After that my only concern was the safety of my daughter. It was unreal."

"Guys, we've been over this. No need to harass the lady." It was Miller protesting. She resisted his assistance.

"Rykov worked for an international trading company. Talk to his employers."

This startled Smith who gave an odd grin.

"International trading company? Rykov told you this?"

"Yes, this morning when I commented on his security; there were threats from some Middle East terrorist group, he said."

The door opened and Caroline veered round, thinking they were bringing Mary. An orderly steered a blood-drenched man in a wheelchair through the doorway. The eyes of the pulped-up face stared at the group. Discovering his mistake, the orderly whipped the man around. This elicited a soft moan when the wheelchair bumped into somebody out in the corridor. When the door closed, the cramped atmosphere became harder to bear. She had allowed an unknown nurse to take her child away. She lost the trail of her thoughts in the rising anxiety. They were taking too long with Mary.

"Mr. Rykov told you this?" The agent prompted her gently.

"Ah, yes, company policy."

"You have no idea who this man was?"

"Yes, I do, Aleksei Rykov, I told you. What do you mean?"

"The old man controlled the most influential criminal organization in the world, and a financial empire that gave him great pull in Washington. We have every reason to believe that his industrial businesses had deep criminal connections. You had no prior knowledge of this man?"

"I don't believe a word of it," said Caroline.

"Aleksei Ivanovich Rykov is a name in a passport. He used it for decades in the Soviet Union. The man was the head of the original Russian Mafia. He was as bad as they come."

Agent Smith looked at the Metropolitan detective. They were feet apart in the cramped room. He was aware that the Bureau had opened a file on Miller who enjoyed mingling with shady foreigners and liked to spend money beyond his means. The Bureau had passed information to Internal Affairs weeks ago. It was early days.

"Rykov was never indicted, here or in Russia. We only have indices that surface at times, you know, corpses popping up in the Dnjepr or the Anacostia. He was a ruthless man."

"There's a two-arm habit for you," said the lieutenant with a merry shrug of disbelief, "you believe the old geezer, running with the Washington campaign crowd and heading the Russian Mafia." He ignored their disapproving stares and grinned at Caroline,

"Maybe the old guy had a soft spot for a beautiful woman," said Smith, almost as an afterthought. "Anything you want to tell us?"

"For Heaven's sake," Caroline smiled nervously down at him. The follow up question had obliterated the compliment.

"I did not know the man. If Krupskaya was his biological daughter, it would suggest he was sexually active years ago? Do I look that desperate?"

Miller turned to the agents. "You, being profilers and him being a gangster, wouldn't he have more success with teenage prostitutes than chasing after Washington widows?"

"I had to ask," Smith murmured with grin she was unable to return. She took him on instead.

"Agent Smith, refresh my powers of deduction. Is my research into the causes of cancer a crime now? Why would the head of a vast crime syndicate give his blood money to medical research?"

"You got me there."

"And I can tell you another truth, as a parent. There was not an evil bone in his body. Everybody could see how he adored his daughter."

Ambushed by rising apprehension Caroline was no longer sure.

"Was Krupskaya his daughter," she asked feebly, but her inner turmoil against this question had her fearing for her own sanity. Of course, she was his daughter.

"The DNA will tell."

Caroline glanced at Miller. His irritating smugness set off another surge of despair.

"This morning, when you saw him off, where was his driver?" Smith shifted tactic.

"In the driver's seat! Why are they taking so long?"

"This is important, Caroline," the small one rebuked her.

It was odd how Miller's implied and logically flawed threat that she was without protection could seem so reasonable, given the circumstances. The educated part of her tried to hold back but the effort was little help against the breathless panic. Before she knew what she was doing, she had worked her mind into a state. Rounding on the agent, she could not hold back the only question she cared to ask. It rushed out without control.

"What have you done with my daughter," she demanded.

Caught by surprise, they stood like statues and stared at her. Not least when the eminent professor dodged between them to throw open the door to run into the crowded hallway where she slammed into a cot and almost threw the patient off it. The impact bared an abdominal wound, a skin-deep mark of a bungled knife attack. The man wailed as Caroline recoiled.

"Jesus!"

The memory came at her out of the blue, her hands in surgical gloves hoisting a yellow spotted liver from a gaping abdomen. That wound was not superficial. 'Too much bad vodka, Orlov,' she said to the man tied down on the table, screaming in pain. The memory of chucking a live liver into a grinder was as natural to her as baking a cake on a Sunday morning. Caroline stood rooted in the corridor, gently swaying.

"Jesus," she repeated as Smith caught up to seize her by the arms, her eyes gazing bewildered into thin air.

"There is something wrong with me."

The Federal agent watched her uncertainly.

"Breathe! Try to calm down." He gave her a moment. "Look Caroline, Mary was the same age as Krupskaya. Maybe that's why Rykov took interest. As you said, his daughter needed a friend. I don't think that your daughter is in any danger whatsoever."

The thought confused her. She closed her eyes to get a grip, regretting the outburst. Miller sauntered over, shaking his head over her disturbing excursion.

"Did anybody leave the scene after the shooting?", asked Smith.

"You way out of line, sonny," Miller protested, "you are messing with her mind. She in shock, having a meltdown. The holes in her story are big enough to fuck sideways. She got opinions, being Professor and all, but she saw no shooter. Everything says it's a drive-by. It will be in my report."

"Ask his bodyguard," said Caroline, pouncing on the first clear thought that struck her.

"The female bodyguard and male driver were both shot dead."

Instantly she realized where the flaw lay.

"Galina, yes, and Pavel, but you ask Boky, Galina's partner."

She had barely uttered the words when she woke to their meaning. What was she saying? She looked down on agent Smith and took in the sharp stab of suspicion.

"Galina, Pavel, Boky? You knew these people by name?"

This threw her into a different confusion.

"I think Rykov called out."

"To all three of them by name?"

"I never saw these people before in my life."

"Can you describe this Boky character?"

"Caucasian male, all muscles and impersonal eyes, handsome," she eyed agent Smith up and down, taking her time about it.

"Tall," she said.

"Where was this Boky when the hit came down?"

"Standing over the dead blonde, Galina. I was down on the asphalt by the old man. I signaled to Boky that he was dead."

"How did you do that?"

"I shook my head."

"Was this other bodyguard taking cover at the time?"

"No, standing tall, surveying the scene."

What was worse, Caroline knew exactly why Boky was not taking cover, growing wary of her own perceptions. Lieutenant Miller was right; she had nothing to gain by getting involved in this mess.

"How long after the shooting was this, you think?"

"A minute or less."

"Was he looking around, trying to figure it out?"

"He was watching us."

"An inside hit," Smith hesitated. He studied her doubtfully before he pulled a dog-eared photo from his leather wallet.

"Ever seen this man before?"

The photo startled her. She took a step backwards in the crowded hallway and bumped into a wounded male who started to rebuke her but backed off when he saw the company she was keeping. The snap showed the face from her vision a moment earlier.

It was the face of her old friend Orlov who she could recall under many circumstances to which she could not possibly be privy. In the last one, Orlov was crying because she was removing his foot.

"Who is this man," she whispered inaudibly, to win time. She recalled that his toenails were yellow and thickened by nail fungus. As a medical doctor, she also knew that some months of Sporonox taken orally would have cured him of the fungus, given that his liver was in good enough shape to cope with the poison, and she had seen his liver.

"You don't need to know that to answer my question," Smith declared confidently but caved in quickly when she kept her silence.

"Orlov is the name, a Russian general fighting Rykov for control. We know he arrived on a private jet through National four days ago. Have you seen this man?", he prompted gently.

Angrily, Miller snatched the mug shot but Junior snatched it right back.

"I don't think so," she said and faltered in her train of thought. Had she told a lie? She was no longer sure. She knew a lot about that butchered old man, a life's worth of information and party business in their old Soviet days. She was equally certain that they had never met. She was in a bad way.

"Did Mr. Rykov say anything before he died," Smith asked off her uncertain headshake.

"No, yes," Caroline fought to gather her thoughts. They seemed to be roaming all over.

"Was that yes? That's not what you told me," Miller growled and shook his head in frustration.

"Not that way. He asked me to touch him."

"To touch him," asked Smith. It was clear he had no take on the significance of that evidence, and neither, it seemed, had she.

"Yes."

"I see. And did you?"

"I reached out for his hand. It was so sad."

"I understand."

"I don't think you do. We had both collected so much static that when our fingers touched, a spark flew between us." Caroline raised a trembling hand and studied a small globular blister on her finger.

"The old man went out like a candle."

"Does this Boky character know who you are?", asked Smith.

"No reason why," she replied too quickly, catching her mind thinking the opposite. She was doing a lot of that.

"Nobody ever met Rykov twice in one day without him having a hand in setting that up," Smith sounded worried, "we must protect your identity." The small special agent turned to the Metro detective.

"Right, Miller?"

"You are all mad," said Caroline. It was a feeble attempt to persuade her mind that she was sanest of the lot. It did not sound convincing.

"Thing is," drawled Miller, "information's king in this town. The press owns the medical staff in this here hospital. They own the cops on the beat and that's half the population right there. I'm not even counting the perps. You got doctors and nurses and ambulance staff that read the Bible, their Washington Post. If you ask me, cat's out of the bag."

This is when Caroline spotted the self-appointed god with the horse teeth weaving his way down the corridor, pushing a rolling cot. She broke from them excitedly to embrace her daughter.

"I took care of it myself, Dr. Glyn; gave her a sedative to relax her; nothing but a hairline crack in the upper tibia. I brought you copies to study." He handed her a brown envelope.

"Thank you, thank you, and thank you!"

And the god from Culpeper wheeled the cot with Mary past the law enforcement officers into another bigger consultation room. He was going all-out in being of personal service. Mary's face was no longer covered by the sheet. Smith smiled down at the child to cheer her up, but his smile got caught in a waft of some atomic winter. It froze on his face.

None of them except Lieutenant Miller paid any attention to a worried couple that had just stepped out of a side cubicle. "They were sleeping pills," a doctor was telling the couple. "She will be out for hours. We'll transfer her upstairs as soon as we can. You can visit in the morning. Go home now. She'll be fine." When Miller sauntered off, nobody minded his departure.

Miller entered the unlocked side cubicle and found a heavily sedated teenager sleeping on a roller bed. Her face was paler than the white linen. The bare cubicle was so tiny that the lieutenant could stand at the foot of the roller bed and reach behind him to lock the door. His other hand lifted the covers to inspect the girl's lower body with mild disinterest. Pulling a cell phone decorated with four stars; he dialed and waited, switching the phone to his right to be better able to fondle the comatose teenager.

"Dr. Caroline Griffith, general, maiden name Glyn," he said thickly. "Medical Professor, you can read all about her in the Post today. Said she saw nothing. I took her preliminary. Maybe she didn't, but now she's saying something else."

Miller flipped the sheet up to the girl's neck, getting excited about it, trying to hold back.

"Oh, girl, what you go and do that for," he muttered as he listened on the phone. Pulling a condom from his pocket, he bit off the wrapper.

"Sure, I warned her off. And she got the message. Reckon she'll stick to her story. Held up this far. No solid recollection of seeing the shooter. I can try for a drive-by shooting. It won't stick. Them Federal boys turning on the charm and she a sucker, wants to do everybody a favor."

"Sure, anything you want. The Professor got a kid. It can be tricky with them Fibbies nosing around."

Head and shoulders turned on the pillow, not of the teenager's own volition. Miller's head came back to counter the thrust of his pelvis.

"A real soft mouse if you ask me."

The burly man went about his deed in the disinterested way of a man stroking his dog. There was a hot lump building in his throat. He had to clear it.

"Ummh, this Boky character! Your asset, is he? Should've trained him better; guy walked around without a care in the world. Professor told us. Reckon he gave the game away. Fibbies think he's the shooter. Yea, sure, she called him Boky. She knew all their names. How about that?"

The white freckled marble head moved rhythmically on the pillow. A string of saliva from the corner of a mouth flecked the white cover and Miller's voice was growing huskier.

"Ummh, you bet, word's out! Was an inside hit."

His head tipped forward; soggy eyes shut in a private dream. He needed the rush. He kept his right hand on the slender body to keep from throwing her. The bulk and power of his movement in the tight space was palpable, his voice fighting to stay controlled.

"If Boky your shooter, you don't wait for Justice to beat down the door, you hear. Get your comrade out of the country." He sounded angry with the heavy breathing. The gangling body on the cot moved violently, then took one last plunge and fell still.

"Whoof, yeaahh. Nothing, general, a fifteen-year-old with an ass you would not believe, tighter than ticks."

Miller tipped down his head to remove the condom. One could not be too careful these days. He listened attentively, mind on more important matters. He drew a vague thud, throwing his load into a covered metal bin. A good solid shot all around.

"If you ask me, general, why not give them Boky?"

He threw a couple crumpled paper napkins into the trash bin to cover up the potentially incriminating contents. Nobody in his right mind would sift through that garbage, let alone try to prosecute an unlikely crime, if any had been committed.

"Sure, they buy it. He's their only lead. The Fibbies already suspect the guy. They love to solve cases. If you help them out, don't mess him up, you hear. The Professor's got to recognize him. If she does, everyone will be happy."

"Right, right, I hear you." He pocketed the small phone and gave a contented sigh. "Commie asshole," he grinned at the girl.

Miller covered her up, took a last look around, unlocked the door and stepped back into the crowded corridor. As luck would have it, he was in time to meet a distraught Caroline and two agents in the company of a red-bearded doctor. The group came ambling out of a consultation room. Miller was partial to red hair; pleased would be the word, tucking his docile tool into position with a satisfying buzz in the can. The commie general had one upside; wealthy enough to set the gold standard, and this was a generous guy.

"A couple of days of hospital care will do Mary a world of good. Three or four days would be better," the doctor reminded Caroline. He would be there for her. Dr. Alice Christian was waiting in the corridor, embracing her, handing over a clean set of clothes.

"Your daughter needs to rest," the doctor persisted, "let us give her a few days of proper hospital care on the upper floors. Trust me;

it will do her a world of good." Caroline realized that even young gods need to feel appreciated. Irritated by her own uncalled-for sarcasm, she chose to affirm.

"You are right, thank you. She'll need to sleep and rest after this."

"I need a guard detail outside her door," said Smith.

"We short on men, but, sure, said Miller generously. "I'll see to it."

"Let me sit with her tonight," Alice Christian pleaded. "You'll feel better in the morning. Go home and rest, and don't touch a telephone." She was a true friend in need. Alice could be trusted.

"Call me, if there's anything, any time," Smith handed her a card. Caroline glanced at Lieutenant Miller who smelled his fingers. She found him unexpectedly flushed and relaxed.

"You can pick him up at Carter's anytime," Miller smiled back. "Couple of shots of bourbon and he's packed. Reckon he can afford to drink himself blind every night. There fringe benefits in being economy size."

Smith let it ride but she saw the withering glance he shot at Miller and loved him for it. Junior loomed above them like a menacing cloud.

"Carter's," she smiled questioningly, studying the card as a nurse wheeled a comatose teenager out from the next-door cubicle. Miller grinned broadly as the cot passed.

"There fringe benefits in everything."

On the steps of Georgetown Hospital, the two agents thanked Caroline for her cooperation. They waited on the steps to watch her drive off in a Saab convertible with the top folded back.

"What do you make of her kid," asked Parker, "the Rykov kid in the morgue could be her daughter."

"Yeah, that was spooky."

"So, what are we missing?"

CHAPTER 6

C AROLINE SPOTTED THEM up ahead and shuddered at the questions they were waiting to ask. She saw TV vans in front of her house with paparazzi spilling out of her driveway. They had been there for hours, littering the leafy street. She had seen these interviews a thousand times in the guise of a shouting match, performed on the run. In fragile condition, it was an appalling prospect. She had seconds to decide. Could she gatecrash some of the neighborhood parties? She made her getaway on squealing tires, turning into the well-proportioned parking lot of the Lehman family.

Most of the guests had already arrived. Dinner was impending. The magnificent neoclassical residence of yellow stucco was humming. She parked on the grass. Eugenia the perfectionist would bug her about it, but she'd be thrilled to have her with the Washington Post article fresh off the presses, crammed with private tidbits. It was no great loss that she would not get to discuss her favorite topic over dinner tonight. They rarely understood what she was talking about. Being stuck with a bore was better than spending an early night in bed alone, and Mary would be spending the night in Georgetown Hospital.

"Caroline, you came. That's the spirit. We heard about the drive-by-shooting". Phillip broke from a small throng to greet her, proud of his timing, catching her early this morning.

She realized there was no escape. News traveled fast in this city. Tonight, she would be called on to explain what she did not understand. It was proper. Caroline was strangely amused. If murder through the ages was man's favorite pastime; the art of explaining what he did not understand was a close runner-up.

Eugenia, Phillip's wife, and tireless warhorse, fell on her like a long-lost friend in sheer enthusiasm. Eugenia was in her early fifties; skin stretched from top and bottom like a bass drum. Her style of coiffure went out with Pamela Churchill Harriman, but careful paintwork accented an unremitting smile. A great panderer to other people's vices and weaknesses, Eugenia threw these bashes every other day. She had her pick of the powerful and the self-important. Written invitations went out weeks in advance, and that made spontaneity hard to come by. Caroline suspected that her hostess considered it a minor victory to have Dr. Glyn-Griffith, the talk of DC at her table tonight.

"Everybody is here, darling. You are even bigger news than the bombing of that hideous train station. We don't like talk of terrorists; they are so terribly boring. I am seating you next to Paul McPherson, the new editor of the Georgetowner. And Dan Rayburn has been asking about you. He is too old for you, but he is here with his old confidante; you know Senator Greenbaum, darling, six foot one and single."

"I am not that desperate, Eugenia."

"A match made in heaven, darling. Dinner is served."

A few dark lounge suits were in evidence among the black and white dinner jackets. The occasion wasn't rigidly formal. Caroline smoothed the striped skirt Alice brought to Georgetown Hospital. It was straight to the point and fitting for a woman who was being served as dessert. To this crowd, she was merely that something extra to cleanse the taste buds after the main course, exotic to the palate but of no great weight.

During dinner, her table companion was Paul McPherson, the new editor of the Georgetowner. She rather liked the man who pushed hard to set her up for an exclusive interview; a firm-jowled Washington face shaped by sound bites and hors d'oeuvres.

"I might, Paul, if the FBI doesn't object. They don't like the publicity. I always thought that was their forte. They don't want me to talk to the press, so if I give you an exclusive, there's a catch," she added, feeling devious.

"You find the charm of light in the shadows," said Paul.

"The media people are camping on my porch."

"Yes, some of them are mine."

"Could you spread the word that I have left town?"

"Our hero wants to hide from the press," the editor lifted the folded linen napkin from his butter plate to dab a smile. "This may be a first in Washington; come to think of it, it may be against the law."

Paul McPherson watched the self-contained faces around the long candlelit table and flashed a smile across the low centerpiece for the benefit of eagle-eyed Eugenia, always the perfect host. So much forethought in her seating charts.

"It is unethical, of course," McPherson swallowed deeply of the vintage red, "but head office can't afford to keep our lens-men loitering. They are a rough bunch, Caroline, more stubborn than wise. I dare say the levelheaded may leave but the paranoids smell a conspiracy in the weather report."

"I could give them a lead to follow."

"What would that be?"

"You know Patrick Miller of the metropolitan police?"

"Yes, Lieutenant of Detectives, a helpful man."

"Suppose I asked him to spread an innocent lie for me; I am attending the three-day medical conference in New York. Would that do it, you think. I'm sure he would not mind."

"Why would he not mind, I wonder?"

"Miller doesn't want me to talk to the press either."

"What an interesting evening this is. I think I will have a word with Miller after we talk. He's a great one for gossip. I dare say it might work."

After dinner, mingling in the ballroom of the Lehman house, she adjusted her technique to the number of people. Each received a smooth delivery of a few lines and a deeply sad personal smile. It had been a long time and she was single and beautiful. She felt curiously at ease among the men. The old breed still got away with puffing cigars after dinner, thinking it was their world. They discussed who had died and what inheritance had been squandered. The young breed was as comforting to study; extroverted tacticians surfing the fluid waves of political coalitions. It was as if she had undergone a transformation and she liked her new cold detachment. It cleared her gaze and gave a welcome absence of emotional contact. The insight pleased her until she realized that this was the way she studied rats.

"There was blood everywhere! Yes, Krupskaya, Mary's best friend. We called her Babushka. It was devastating. They killed her father; Aleksei Ivanovich, a kind old man, well, a certain dryness of heart, but I only met him this morning. Now the FBI insists that he controlled the Russian Mafia. What nonsense!"

She enjoyed mingling, more than she remembered, launching this mantra in assorted shades upon respectful guests. Unlike the newshounds on her porch, the socialites never hooked you with hard follow-up questions. She felt unusually snug and safe to be fawned over by strangers with embraces and kisses for nothing she said. For being there; an exotic plant in the vanity turf of a professional ego. To be doted on by powerful peers was more pleasant that she remembered, a dried flower for the scrapbook. If she ever managed to become a certified saint of medicine, her name would crop up in the memoirs, the crowning goal of any careerist. Caroline caught her mind thinking in this mean-spirited way and she paused to blush for no reason. Taking a deep breath, she made her excuses from a small group after another recital and put in that call to Lieutenant Miller.

When she rejoined the crowd, old Dan Rayburn was holding court with Senator Greenbaum, his confidante during the Chicago days in the Daley machine, now the ranking Democrat on the Senate Intelligence Committee. Tall, broad shouldered and balding in his late sixties; Greenbaum was going to seed despite determined efforts.

He had a thick gravel voice that took no prisoners. Caroline had met him and his friend Rayburn at parties before but the uninvited memories that crowded her head at this moment did not fit any of these occasions.

"Senator Greenbaum."

"Caroline. Heard you had a close scrape today. How are you girl? You remember Dan Rayburn, the industrialist. That's what everybody calls him. All he really does is to practice the well-paid politics of special interests."

"A game older than sin, my dear, but you're so young." The industrialist said this almost resentfully, holding on to a mistress or a grandchild. Dan was a sturdy man with a strong voice and with the cobwebs of age slashed across the slack pouches of aged flesh. When Caroline gave him the smile she practiced in the mirror this morning, she felt curiously at ease with the old man. His was a face speckled by stubborn liver spots that neither lasers nor twenty-year-old beauties could becloud. Many of Dan's companies were major defense contractors. His turf reached far outside the beltway.

The stunning young woman on his arm smiled and moved mirthfully up against old Rayburn. Caroline recalled the famous model from the covers of magazines she rarely picked up and never read. A wonderful fresh face so youthful that it needed no touch of the creams she touted on television or billboards throughout the country. Caroline watched the pair of full pink lips and sensed a flutter of sexual confusion. The girl was strikingly attractive. Trying to reign in her imagination, she felt unaccountably hot. The strange memory of carnally possessing this lively young woman was deeply distracting. Her mind was running on tracks outside her control.

Caroline checked her thoughts. Were these the aftershocks of posttraumatic stress? All these pictures in her mind could not be actual memories. Yet their clarity and sense of purpose were not disorganized. It contradicted all University lectures she had attended on the syndrome. This young woman had worked for her, for Rykov. It had nothing to do with research. The girl was paid to keep tabs on Rayburn while secretly two-timing with the Senator. Her name was Tsvetayeva, and Caroline knew how to spell it in both English and Cyrillic.

"Marie Luise von Ettersberg," Dan Rayburn boomed as he introduced his favorite trophy.

Caroline gasped at the touch of her hand. She, or rather Rykov, had brought her here as a Lithuanian emigrant with a false identity and a valid passport to prove it. It was Rykov's ploy to explain her almost inaudible Russian accent. Unable to meet her sincerely joyful eyes, Caroline focused on baby smooth skin as the memory of being alone with Tsvetayeva unfolded. The girl faced her in a black striped suit top, nothing else. It was strangely appealing.

"I am pleased with your film of Senator Greenbaum," Caroline told the girl in fluid Russian, in a deep male voice, inquisitive about her mission.

"Does he like to dress up like that?"

"The Senator is a ballet enthusiast. As you know, that is my specialty, my area of expertise. Made him an easy target."

"This worries me, girl. I did not expect him to fall so fast for Vasily's idea of skimming the Air Force. It is a crude idea. Move carefully!"

"Yes, great lover!"

Caroline laughed out loud, unwilling to let go of her hand. The Senator and Dan exchanged glances, pleased that their prize filly had won another admirer. Caroline knew that the girl was not playacting in her memory. Held in terror, her servility knew no bounds. Whatever she asked, this girl would do. Caroline had killed several youngsters in her presence on separate occasions for the sole purpose to impress on Tsvetayeva the value of duty, all carefully planned to modify her behavior and reinforce the value of following her command. She was a valuable instrument in his service. At the Lehman party, the girl gave her new fan a brilliant smile, but Caroline still didn't let go her hand. The voice in her head refused to be silent.

"I am pleased with your tapes, little Tsvetayeva. They may be of use later. Your dismissal of the Senator's decaying physique is due to inexperience. He is still able to muscle some of the savviest power brokers in Washington. Never question his clout."

"Yes, my God!"

"The senator thinks that it was his sexual prowess that caused you to betray old Rayburn. Keep him thinking that. Your devotion to old Rayburn must be complete; can he still get it up?"

"If I work hard, powerful lover!" Caroline suppressed another outburst of laughter. This was ridiculous.

"Come, show me child."

Caroline blinked in confusion as Tsvetayeva advanced on her and slipped to her knees. The games played by the old and powerful.

When she opened her eyes, it pleased her for the briefest of moments that Tsvetayeva was shaking her hand and nothing else. Holding her hand was embarrassing but the sojourn was short lived. The memories kept coming.

"So, little Tsvetayeva, did your mission to seduce the honorable Dr. Robert Kingsley Griffith succeed?" Caroline knew that her levelheaded questions in another language were no alternate reality. They were genuine.

"Umh, yes my Lord!"

"He tried on your tight warm gloves?"

"Yes, oh yes."

"All three?"

"Two, and he needed convincing."

It was all going to Caroline's head that was now scarlet. She felt her heart hammering in her chest.

"Did the good Doctor sleep afterwards?"

"Umh, yes, Master! I put the container next to his head and released the radiation shield for thirty minutes, as you ordered."

"Excellent. That gives him a few weeks."

Surely Ivanovich did not have her husband killed? Caroline knew with uncanny clarity that it was precisely so. In the past year, her friends and family had died in a clever string of assassinations. She lost it.

"Excuse me," she gasped in open panic and broke away from the Senator and his group, aiming broadly at the nearest door, gaining the distance in too few steps. Tsvetayeva dropped her released hand and the well worked smile wavered. Her new fan was seeking shelter in the public bathroom of the Lehman residence. The girl looked up at Dan, shaking his head in wonder as Caroline rushed across the marble floor. It was a scene unfit for the catwalk. Dan pointed with his head and the model followed in her calm poise.

Caroline stood heaving, trying to control her breathing. She took hold of the shining marble basin with both hands to seek support, head down. She threw water in her face. The drumbeat faded slowly.

The water, like her daughter's breakfast went astray. She straightened up to study the mirror; she was a sight. Water in her hair. Water flecks on the front of her striped two-piece. What a fool she was. She had to clean up before the curious picked up the trail. She set to work with a paper towel. The guests out there expected a famously stoic scientist, not a nervous wreck.

She hardly heard the door when Tsvetayeva entered, locking it behind her, probably hoping for the exclusive rights to her new fishing trip.

"Mrs. Glyn-Griffith, are you all-right?"

In the mirror, Caroline focused for a moment on the young woman behind her, shifting back to an infinitely sorrier sight. What a mess she was. That other track in her mind made a Herculean effort to stem her feelings but she was stronger than him. This young filly had baited a honey trap for her husband. A violent burst of anger got the better of her. It exploded in her head and swept away what remained of her infamous cool. That was never more than window dressing anyway. She turned in headless fury and waded in, like a lioness on the prowl. The prey was the young gazelle her husband had pronged in her extravagant illusion. Her fist connected and she caught a flimsy fabric of a blouse on the rebound. Ripping as she might, she saw rather than heard the buttons fly.

"Damn you little Tsvetayeva," she hissed, panting from the effort. Caught off balance, the stunned girl shielded her valuable face more in fright than anger, because of the words. She pushed the older woman with her elbows up against the marble washbasin. Caroline let up; her heart was no longer in it. They stood inches apart, staring at each other, panting. Tsvetayeva had developed a hefty nosebleed and Caroline watched her with a cruel mixture of pleasure and humiliation.

"My bogus Lithuanian emigrant."

"Who are you?"

"Dosing his head with radiation makes you a murderer."

"What are you talking about," the girl whimpered.

"You murdered my husband."

"How do you know these things?"

Despite a trembling voice, the implications of her foolish response dawned on Caroline. How could any of this be true? For a moment she tried to review her hallucinations but got tangled up in mean-spirited strands that merged in her mind. With nowhere to go and nothing to say, she let escape an unrestrained bawl. Another part of her marveled how pitiful it sounded compared to her favorite screamers in the Anacostia Asylum for the Criminally Insane. Overwhelmed by fathomless self-pity, Caroline, cut off her crying.

"Who are you?" the girl repeated, "I follow orders. You know that."

"I am Rykov!" Caroline smudged her tears and smiled horribly until anger and spontaneous hatred got the better of her. She wanted to hurt the girl for her evil deed. The other part wanted to reward her.

"What?"

"What, my great lover. Say it!"

"What, my great lover?" The tone was sheer desperation. The petrified little animal was trying to sift through her appalling past for some rational explanation. Her breathless panic was showing.

"Did you work for him?" There was hope in those Bambi eyes. They begged for affirmation.

"You thought I was dead, little Tsvetayeva. It would suit you to enjoy your lifestyle without any duty to me. How brave you are to betray me. I took your best girlfriend apart as a warning to you. You were not this brave then, making clumsy love to me while she sung for you. How quickly you forget."

The hope died in the Bambi eyes.

"I need to know that you are still mine."

"I'd die for you, great leader, even like that, if you wish." The claw like nails raised to full lips trembled so wildly that it was almost comical.

Shaking her head in angry denial, Caroline groped behind her on the washstand. Her hand came across a heavy jar and chucked it at the girl with all her might. The jar went hurling through the air in the general direction of Tsvetayeva who ducked with the agility of youth. It bounced off the mahogany door with a crash that could stop a rave party, then smashed into the marble wall like a perfect closure. The girl closed her eyes to block out hair gel and flying glass. It was over.

"There will be no ducking next time, damn you. Your task is to work on Dan and Greenbaum. Wait for my command." The measure of kindness in her hoarse voice took them both by surprise. "Get out. Take your tight warm gloves with you."

"Yes, my perfect mistress. Call for me. I will be good for you in your new body, whatever you demand."

And with these words, a bloody and battered Marie Luise von Ettersberg bolted in unearthly fear out of a bathroom to run across a floor in a tattered blouse. Dan Rayburn received her aghast and had to fight the Senator from fawning over his trophy.

Every eye of the large party was fixed on the doorway to the ballroom toilet. The distinguished crowd hung on the edge of silence. Nobody even moved. The hushed sobs of the teen supermodel had all their ears.

Eugenia Lehman walked boldly to the bathroom door, for the first time this evening without a smile. The steely character of the older woman was out in the open for all to see. As she closed the door on the crowd, more than anything, her concern was for a friend. She embraced the tear-streaked vision that was Caroline.

"What happened, darling?"

"I snapped. I don't have an explanation."

"What did the little tart say to you?"

"She had an affair with Robert."

"Darling, Robert was not that kind. We went way back, you know that. I recall that he did attract the odd girl. That was before your time. You are not thinking straight."

"You're right. Must be the murder I witnessed today."

"Go home and lie down, darling. You look like a battered housewife. Give me five minutes to clear the front room. You can slip away unseen. We don't want any of them to see you like this."

"I can't hide, Eugenia. Not after this. But you are right, I am going home."

"Are you up to facing them, darling; you look a mess."

She turned to a brilliant mirror that allowed no ignorance. Eugenia was right. It would take her half an hour to put this passably right. And passable wasn't her style.

As she embraced Eugenia, she was touched by the lack of substance in her bird-like skeleton so cleverly veiled by a will of iron.

As Caroline boldly pulled open the heavy door, she faced a wall of people and silence. The high-octane hum that circled the ballroom stopped as if somebody had thrown a switch. She could have heard a pin drop.

There was nothing to do but the perfect performance.

Caroline set a defiant course straight into the gawking crowd with head high and shoulders back, assuming ease. She did not look, as if they were not there.

It would later be said that her unwavering walk across that large floor to the front foyer showed great inner strength while her outward appearance reflected vulnerability.

The crowd parted before her like the Red Sea.

From the bathroom doorway, Eugenia gazed after her young protégé across the expanse left empty in her wake. The older woman appeared exhausted and saddened, almost broken, but as Caroline reached halfway, everybody missed the dawning of a new glorious smile on their hostess. The iron mask closed. As her guests stood like pillars and followed every flawless step across the ballroom floor to the front foyer, none saw the old lady raise a bejeweled fist in proud homage.

"That's my girl," she whispered.

Eugenia Lehman knew it in her bones. Tonight's party had been made. It would go straight into the annals of the Georgetowner as the party of the year. This was the stuff that turns anecdotal gossip into gold. This was a party to remember.

It would last forever.

CHAPTER 7

SHE LEFT HER car in the packed parking lot of the Lehman's and walked home in the warm darkness. Every last reporter had gone. There was a black van with smoked windows and diplomatic plates parked across from her house, probably a spillover from the Lehman bash. Entering, she cut the main lights to avoid interest and repeated her New York conference lie into the answering machine. A growing sense of vulnerability was getting on her nerves. Moving distractedly about the house, she found herself obsessively checking the street, gazing into the darkened driveway. A freak gust of wind sent twigs hurling by a lamppost. Everything alarmed her. She peered into the road at the shiny black van parked by the curb. Was it bad suspension or something more sinister that caused that gentle roll?

"What are the kids doing in there," she said aloud, going for a silly compromise to soothe her overwrought mind.

The networks barely mentioned the Georgetown massacre. Without visual impact, it never amounted to more than an appendix to the superior footage from the Union Station bombing. The murder of Aleksei Rykov got tangled up with a gang-fight over prostitution. Lieutenant Patrick Miller of the metropolitan police told the press that a conflict had led to a bungled drive-by shooting. A helpful anchorman found this well suited for a punch line about the ailing capital. Caroline silenced the wailing ambulances.

The telephone purred on the cherry wood sideboard. The machine had run out of memory and was no longer dealing with incoming calls. At the best of times, she seldom returned calls unless they were important to work. Those were the means by which she managed her life. Few bothered to try and that was fine with her. She had no patience with people making demands on her time. She had never called anybody for comfort. If there ever was a need, she knew she'd face the First Law of Thermodynamics; you cannot withdraw what you have not deposited. She had never lent a shoulder for others to cry on. Her account was empty.

It took serious effort to calm her distraught psyche. Whom can you turn to when you can't trust your mind? If this was a mental breakdown, could she impose intellect to resolve the problem? Her hallucinations had felt like memories. She knew they were not. Tsvetayeva's responses signaled something other than post-traumatic stress. Maybe the kid was hooked on drugs? Dating old Dan indicated expensive habits. Could she blame the poor thing for misunderstanding after her unprovoked attack?

Caroline sat listlessly and wondered if she would ever feel alive again, like with Robert. He was provocative, witty, and never demanding, not even on the lecture circuit, or their travels abroad. The physical part of their bond was never dominating. They were two of a kind, pushing on in their field, endlessly talking to colleagues. The talk was great, mostly on cellular mutation. They never got to see the sights. In Venice, they knew the canals by the stink. They knew the restaurants by topics discussed over forgotten meals or by bills kept for expenses.

That look today across a crowded hospital reception, the fleeting gaze of a handsome federal agent. She felt a sudden loss.

What would it be like to fondle a man after all this time? She tried to resist the thought of a lover. Smooth skin on a hard body. Did her faun have anything to offer but the pleasures of the flesh? She tried to think of Robert; recalling a body moving against hers by the open window of a darkened hotel as four eyes roamed out across murky waters in slow pleasure; an unlit canal in Venice. She missed that part of her life so deeply that it hurt. Robert was everything the federal agent was not, and vice versa.

In the bedroom, she made a detour for strength, to touch the face of her framed husband, ashamed of her thoughts. Maybe it was fear. She was touched by that old chill; the sensitivities of youth, that unspeakable fear of the unknown, searching every shadowy corner and listening for the signs of movement. She would have to shore up her defenses. Feeling bone tired, Caroline decanted red port into a cut crystal glass on a polished silver tray. A couple of glasses make her drowsy. She knew that the reporters would lie in wait for her tomorrow at Georgetown Hospital. She would be hounded by a vengeful press for shaking them off.

She rubbed her skin with a coarse Turkish towel after the steamy shower and enjoyed ta sensuous feeling of skin, open and heavy. It did not reclaim the intimacy lost with her husband. She studied her face in the surround light from the bedroom mirror, a dangerous trait. She always liked what she saw. No spring chicken, but beautiful, her faun had offered. The world had changed since her youth, especially for the young generation. Unbroken spirits were in short supply. Looking back on her life, she wanted Mary to find the urge to engage with the world. God knew there were enough problems to solve. The Church of Science protected their turf by using complexity to blur the big picture. It intimidated the young.

Cheated them out of their birthright. When you put up hurdles against youthful curiosity, you allow leaders to harness strength for hidden agendas, the biggest game in town.

Caroline tried to emerge her mind in these abstract thoughts to keep that other ugly strand at bay. It was scary to suspect your mind of duplicity. Even her sexual confusion at Lehman's was deeply upsetting, imagined or not. She wondered if she could seduce her faun. Was she still able to perform these acts? She put on silk pajamas and paced the floor in dread, heart jumping at every sound.

"The tree, stupid," she told the living room as a rasping sound carried through the house. That damn branch was rubbing against the drainpipe again.

It was too early for sleep. By her desk in the study, sipping port in the half dark, she studied her three small handwritten pages of formulas from yesterday. Why had she laid them out in the wrong order, the last page on top?

"That's a bit cavalier, mixing up the math?" She shook her head, trying to make the rearranged pages into an accidental mistake. Don't do this, she begged of her mind. The order of the pages would not be clear to an amateur. Somebody had gone through her papers. Was he still in her house? She blinked in sudden alarm as she spotted it. The desk slot that held the file on Roberts's cancer was empty. Her privately compiled, by now extensive data on his mysterious tumor was not there. These tumors were normally linked to direct doses of heavy radiation. The file was gone. That threw her. That and the horrible thought of Robert asleep with Tsvetayeva as she released the radiation shield. She flinched from a shadow that moved across the curtain in her study but forced a sustained look until another sheaf of leaves danced into the streetlight. A car door slammed. This was not going to be an easy night.

When another hurried gulp of port did little to soften the shiver, she put the empty glass down so high-handedly it almost cracked. It was hard to fight aberrations with rationale. The perverse, white-knuckled panic sneaked up and overwhelmed her. She fled into the bedroom where a bedside lamp cast its warm light on the pillows. The familiar stacks of research literature soothed her. In the dead stillness, she burrowed under the covers as indefinable fear spread through her, spilling into open alarm, growing like a cancerous tumor, a fascist mutation as advance cells prowled her bloodstream.

A minute later, in epileptic frenzy, she flung off the covers to sprint across the darkened hallway and down the stairs again. She run the short distance to her dining room where she stopped panting inside the doorway to blink away darkness. She peered hard until she made out the high-backed chair, the glint of a glass eye. Yes, she was there.

Caroline snatched the smiling rag doll to her bosom and raced back to the bedroom to dive under the covers a second time. Hugging the doll fiercely, she pulled the covers over her head. Babushka was the only one she could protect in this house. And with a child to protect, a mother could withstand any evil, ward off any fear.

"Don't be afraid. Mommy's here," she whispered under the covers. It was a controlled soothing voice. It was early evening. Out in the dark street, the black van glittered ominously.

Later that night, the wind died down. The trees grew silent. In her bedroom, holding the arm of a smiling rag doll, Caroline is asleep. The reading lamp is. The covers are on the floor. Face down in a strange bed, she raises her head to the view from an open window, eyes roaming the dark waters of an unlit Venice canal, dreaming. She listens to the water lap at the wall beneath their window. By the hushed murmur of the bedsprings, she melts into Roberts's body moving in her. Caroline moans and turns over on her bed, holding on to the rag doll.

There is a change of setting. A man with a lion's mane steps out from behind the great oak. An aid jumps to open the limousine door. A gray head ducks into a gray car.

And then, Rykov is dreaming through older eyes, walking that young Dr. Glyn Griffith, down the winding path.

"There must be a misunderstanding..."

He lets go of Babushka's arm to study young Caroline. The plan is in place. But there is a rumble from a distant explosion. He runs from her out the gate. His painful breathing is a drumbeat. Two hollow shots ring out. He punches Galina out of his way. Pavel is down on the asphalt on top of that other kid. Running heavily towards the limousine, only Babushka on his mind. Has his daughter been hit? Hoisting her limp body, he knows this is a wrong move. It is too late. What an astounding ending; caught in a trap sprung by love.

This is good, Caroline thinks in his mind; he cannot be all bad. What it this girl doing in his mind? He needs no redemption from her to wash away the achievements of an extraordinary life. His heart rises against her weakness. With a stupid stocking over his head, Kuznetsov takes careful aim; a traitor pissing his pants.

If he fails, there is nowhere to hide from Aleksei Ivanovich. This Ukrainian peasant isn't even Russian and thinks of himself as a poet. The monochrome vision is in slow motion. Rykov swivels his head to Boky, holstering his gun after killing Galina. This is his trusted man, now standing at ease behind the American doctor as he scurries towards her daughter, she too blinded by love. Boky no longer sees him as a threat. It does not take much to betray a man who gave you a life and protected your family? How much is loyalty worth? The art of betrayal is in the genes that corrupt all but steel. Rykov is pure steel.

He tries to let go of Babushka but is too later. Kuznetsov had waited for this moment. He would inherit an empire. From the corner of an eye, he sees fire spit. His mind registers hollow spatter, but no sounds. The heavy kicks to his chest are the jolts of impact. The lead has already passed through Babushka. Thrown against the limousine grille, he drops his child. She tumbles to the ground. In the chrome, he spots the tortured reflection of a demoted general with a stocking over his head. Even now the coward is unsure if his master can reach out. They had grown up with his power. The panic is clawing at his mind, tearing at him like the slugs in his chest. His time is up.

The young American woman had given her word, a solemn pact for life and beyond. Steps were in place to secure her future.

"He killed my, my...?"

His old lungs seize to breathe. It is less painful that way. He holds on to his last gasp of air to speak, as the young doctor reaches for Babushka's head.

"Your daughter is dead."

It took character to say it simply. This young woman would be his arm. He fights for the words. There is no air. There is no time.

"Our pact, remember .... Touch me!"

The splendid creature shies away.

"What," she whines.

The panic in him explodes. He is angry. It keeps him from slipping away. There is no time to explain. No air to speak.

"Touch me!"

Then he sees the sign. It is a powerful sign, the last vision of a long spectacular life. Young slender fingers reach to carry him over. He fights to focus, to gather the will to raise his hand to hers. His vision goes dark from the edges inwards, sucking all light into a central vortex. The bright point implodes into a brilliant spark of wonderful radiance, and then, empty blackness.

In bed, in her Tenley house, Caroline Glyn wakes up disoriented. The rag doll slips to the floor. The bulb on her reading lamp grows many times brighter and starts to whisper like an angry bee.

'Bzzzzhhz,' it says, and goes out.

"Shit!"

It is pitch dark, but her misgivings have passed. Picking the covers from the floor, sweeping on a silk nightgown, she feels rested. In the living room, she tosses down a brimful of Port in a solid gulp, refilling the glass. Strangely, the fear is gone.

There is no room for fear if you are in total control. Caroline shakes her head and walks back into the dusky bedroom where she flicks on the lights round the dressing table mirror. The night is young. The time had come to freshen up. Sliding onto the cushioned seat, she prepares a smile for a sleep-rumpled face in the mirror. As her reflection moves onto the glass, the massive shock makes it impossible to breathe.

The top of her head glitters above the gray well-groomed sideburns. The reflection in the mirror is that of an old man, the image of Aleksei Ivanovich Rykov. In the mirror, Rykov shakes his head at the absurdity of this sight.

"Shit," says her voice.

'Shit,' mouths the mask in the mirror.

In shock, inch above the cushion, she shuts her eyes, half crouching. Opening them to look down on tightly knit fingers on the dressing table. They are her hands. She sits down heavily and buries her head in these hands like a baby who wants the bad to go away. It took a while to dig up the courage for another look. What brought her round was the comical reflection lodged on her retina, a haggard old man in a pink nightgown. She shakes her head, forcing a second look. Her reflection is back to normal, all lit up, clear as day, removing her hands from her eyes.

"That was worse than Hoover in drag," she murmurs to the mirror, following the lips mouthing these words at her through the glass, forcing them to smile at a simile she did not understand.

"I'm cracking up."

The forced smile prevented the well-groomed mask from returning. She put on lipstick, sensing discomfort from an alter ego, pausing to sip port, as she put on white bra and cotton trousers. The earrings and pearls looked lovely against her skin. As an act of defiance against the madness, she tried to concentrate her mind on target. Could agent Carl Smith anchor her mind? Rummaging through her purse, she inspected the calling card he handed her at Georgetown Hospital.

"I need a man," she whispered.

She called from her study to give the FBI operator the same message.

As she walked across to pick up her Saab in the Lehman parking lot, she glanced at the diplomatic red-white-and-blue plates of the black van.

She knew deep down that despite its faulty suspension, what was in the works behind its shaded windows, the van implied no threat.

CHAPTER 8

R ACING DOWN WISCONSIN Avenue was miraculously easy without heavy daytime traffic. Passing Key Bridge into Virginia, the alcohol made Caroline comfortable enough to unbuckle her seat belt. Coasting down George Washington Memorial Parkway, the warm wind tangled strands of her hair, mirroring the airplane lights above her, banking towards National on the Potomac. Not once did she look in the rearview mirror to study her face.

She did not dare.

It was close to midnight. Special agent Smith had returned her call within minutes. She had suggested Carter's, his after-work hangout. There was that natural fragrance that appealed to lovers in the streets. Putting up the top, she found a parking space off Duke Street. The Old Town cobblestones felt reassuring under her sneakers, worn to give him the edge. Music spilled out of hidden establishments, hard-edged rock and reggae, uneven as the cobblestones. Creole Jazz mingled freely with Irish songs and Louisiana Cajun.

Housed among familiar hometown Alexandria in a cellar and marked by a small nondescript sign, the small redneck bar on Pitt Street was easy to locate. It lay below a fashionable art gallery with a display you could not miss. The window held a brilliantly lit glass enclosure filled with formaldehyde. Submerged in its middle, a pink pig drifted in the liquid with what seemed a blissful smile. Caroline watched the pig for a long moment.

"Believe me", she mouthed, "I know how you feel".

Carters was a small place with a big bar and some dimly lit tables, a serious drinking establishment with imitation wood on the walls and no live music. From an old jukebox came the haunting sound of bluegrass. No dancing. It was an unlikely pickup dive for a mostly male clientele that didn't seem to be gay. Casting around for her faun, she made for the bar. The stags watched the dazzling beauty slide onto her stool as if it were her birthright to command the room. The sneakers made her movements feline. The large mirror behind the bar was the only well-lit spot in the cellar.

"Stolichnaya, neat."

It was a fall-down drink, and fittingly so she thought, smiling vaguely at the bartender, a wafer-thin specimen with transparent skin, sickly enough to augment the gloom.

"You know your poison," he said.

By habit, she glanced in the mirror and averted her eyes. The old man was sitting in her seat, wearing her dress. He glanced her way, vaguely smiling.

"Make that a double."

"Ummhh!" A large swig stiffened her resolve. This was good stuff. She looked around cheerfully. The smiles confirmed that this was an establishment where loneliness could be overcome, or perhaps not with Rykov as chaperone. She had not been out for ages.

It didn't take long. A tall muscular hunk with dark cropped hair in a black embroidered shirt from the Georgetown Hoyas split from a buddy at the bar to hit on her. He came on with the carefree swagger women find attractive in young lovers, the king of the roost swagger that women admire in their sons and despise in old men.

"You better looking than my mum," he offered, appraising her like an athlete preparing for a jump. It was a novel pick up line. She noticed handcuffs back there.

"Mirror, mirror on the wall," she said.

"That's when she was nineteen," he said. "She was Miss Virginia. I'm Tom."

Caroline could tell that Tom knew his way around spirited women of the less guarded sort. They would give him what he did not get from mom. She drained her glass.

"Are the handcuffs for work or fun," she asked with a smile in the mirror. She shouldn't have.

"Department of Justice; I'm with the FBI," he said.

Maybe there were groupies who swarmed for agents. Judging from the clientele down in this watering hole, it was not an effective ploy. For some reason, she knew of hundred places in Washington where the trade of information for a touch of skin was more promising. Trying to listen politely to his advances, she watched the handsome Hoover boy in the mirror buttering up an ancient Soviet diehard in a dress. It broke her up.

"You a stewardess?"

"I'm not your mother," she laughed, shaking her head. It was hard to remain aloof from her hilarious reflection.

"Hit me again," she nodded at the bartender and sighed contentedly when he blocked out the image in the mirror.

The Hoyas hunk was clearly focused on one thing only, if this blonde bombshell was going to blow, it might as well be him. Distasteful as she found that thought, he might be right. She had no idea what to do if her faun did not show. Anything was better than coming apart.

"Win any prices?" he asked, still thinking about his mother.

Tom moved his arm boldly across her shoulder, finger brushing briefly against her collarbone, evaluating her reaction. When there was none, the back of her neck got a firmer repeat. This man is a fine recruit for military command, she thought. Moments later, a hand was playing with her chin, a finger hovering near her lips, inviting a quick bite. Watching all this in the mirror, she had to stifle a scream of frantic laughter. The barkeeper wiped his hands on the spotted cloth around his consumptive frame and turned to his bottles with a shake of his head.

Tom gave a smile, just shy of frustration. She watched him rock old shoulders in the mirror, vaguely threatening without intent, like men in general; telling her to behave.

"You are weird," he said.

"You don't know the half of it."

Nothing came of it. Tom had weighed his chances and let it go. The man was a realist. Nobody this sexy was barhopping at this late hour unless she was damaged goods. Borderline cases were risky. Like most of the guys, he had serious drinking to do. You don't walk away from that for anything less than a sure thing. He pushed away from the bar, almost colliding into another agent who stepped off the stairs.

"What's the matter, Tom," Smith asked off his frustration. The two knew each other.

"Nothing, that beauty at the bar can't stop laughing and I wasn't even being funny."

Smith flashed a smile through the mirror and imagined himself visibly shrinking. The woman was formidably beautiful without giving it a thought. He put a hand on Tom's shoulder and led him away.

"She's the medical professor who witnessed the Georgetown massacre earlier today."

"That's why she's laughing?"

"Dr. Glyn-Griffith asked to meet me here. The Director just assigned the case to me. This is business, Tom."

"A medical professor, huh?"

Through the mirror, beyond her flawed reflection, Caroline watched the two men split up, the hunk returning to his buddy with a shake of his head. Carl sat himself on the abandoned stool beside her.

"What's up with Tom?" he asked quietly. The attraction and his tactful ambivalence helped her regain control.

"You are a regular man's man, Carl." Her voice sounded a trifle drunk.

"Was Tom bothering you?"

"You cannot blame a man for trying." She looked into the glaring mirror and felt drained. "Was his mother a stewardess?"

"You a real hustler, you know; took him two years to tell me that. She died in an airline crash years ago."

"What do you folks do down here," she asked wearily, weighed down by a sudden whiff of boredom. "Are you all waiting for an earthquake?" Tiptoeing around like this was frustrating.

He eyed her warily through the mirror, not missing a beat.

"Yeah, we're all waiting for the Earth to move." Her faun had no shortage of confidence.

"Can we sit away from this damned reflection?"

Carl liked her for the consideration. As he followed her from the bar, she knew that he would notice the sneakers. He would think of a dozen comments and discard them. He did. The dimly lit table had a burned down candle, its wax on the checkered cloth. Carl lit the stump. A man who did not smoke but used a lighter was clearly ready for anything.

"According to the Post," he said, warming to the gleam in her eyes "you may be up for a Nobel Prize," working the Post into the conversation.

"The Post thinks I'm a crooked politician."

"Yes, well, we have a problem with the Washington Post. They got a call from some guy, a Russian immigrant who claims he took part in the Georgetown hit. This guy's willing to testify if we give him protection. The Post thinks the guy's a crackpot. Called us to check his story."

"So where is the problem?"

"From what he said, he must have been there. He had all the details, and with the Post in on it, we can't play down the story. This guy told the paper that you personally saw the hit go down. Now, I'm not saying you did..."

"But?"

"These guys are not to play with."

"Are you?"

"Look, it does not matter if you roll over now."

"I like the sound of that, roll over?"

"If you know things that you are keeping from us. If they suspect you have incriminating testimony, you are in the line of fire."

"I didn't come here to think about this."

"Why did you come?"

"I had a leftover emotion; I thought I might spend it on you."

"I don't think we move in the same circles."

"I need someone to cater for such urges to which the honorable state of matrimony is otherwise ordained."

"Ah, you better run that by me again."

"You may be more familiar with the four-letter word."

"Oh."

"Short and sweet like the man," she said with a flirting gaze. "Could you get me another drink?"

With some reluctance, he brought vodka on the rocks to augment her sagging spirits, watching her nurture the glass in the half-light. It brought her features up to a barely gray tint. The flickering candle underlined a perfect jaw. Her face drew him, red lips breathing the vodka, sailing close to the brim and the murmuring rocks. Caroline knew that he was ready to lose himself, melting with her ice cubes.

"I was thinking, when we bring in this Russian witness, if you can back his story, that would make the story stick. It would let you off the hook. Chances are you can recall him from the scene."

"He is not in custody?"

"No, the people who ordered the hit are after him., so he's scared and careful. We pull him in when he calls back."

"Grow up, Carl. You are here as a messenger. Listen to your message. There is no Russian immigrant. He does not exist. This is a warning to me."

"How you figure?"

"The man sending the message has a copy of my statement. He knows every word I uttered. He is being careful. He is making sure. You tell me the man who wants to talk is now hunted by the Russian mafia. All that is now missing is for the unreal immigrant to turn up dead. That would be the punch line to your message. You are telling me to keep my mouth shut. Not advising me to give evidence."

"How does one do that," he asked gently.

"Do what?"

"Take out a guy who doesn't exist."

"Don't be small-minded too, darling. Since you don't know anything about this man, any dead Russian will do. You'll see. They will help you solve the case; hand you the killer. May not be the right man, but with an airtight case, the bureau will accept the gift and be grateful. This is no low life two-bit conspiracy. This has official backing. You are out of your depth."

He looked at her mournfully and wondered why a female cancer researcher was talking this way.

"I have a feeling you know more than you let on."

"My feeling exactly. Half the time I think I am imagining things."

"Anything you want to tell me?"

Caroline watched him dreamily. The alcohol had a calming effect on her strung nerves.

"I have a problem with that. Let it rest."

"Sure, whenever you are ready. Anything less specific you want to share with me?"

"Besides my bed," the slip embarrassed her more than him.

"Your Director Moffett told me once at a party that Justice was weakened by the war on drugs. He could not even grasp the basics; that the drug cartels are selling risk, that's all they sell; the higher the risk, the greater their profit."

"That's unspecific all right."

"Jacking up the penalty makes them stronger. Ever had the idea that you are serving them, not the rest of us?"

"Thanks for putting me straight."

"You think I have a lively imagination?"

"Sure, you make your living off it. In my line of work, it's called an occupational hazard."

"Trust a man to equate imagination with intelligence."

"Aah, did I?"

"Trust the Department of Justice to consider intelligence an occupational hazard."

"I wouldn't want to have a domestic argument with you."

"I don't do domestics."

"Got your life all staked out then?"

"That's my problem. I don't have a life. I have work and I have Mary. The rest of my family is dead. I cannot grab any opportunity that comes my way without taking a long hard look."

"Know what that sounds like?"

"Greek," she asked sheepishly.

"Grab a guy like me and you might end up living with him."

"What a scary thought," she said, eying the bar. "Would you take me home now," she hesitated, "or is that against the rules?"

Before her eyes, Smith face was turning into a large pink rat with whiskers. She recalled the rat from her dream this morning.

"Stop it!"

Her angry command startled the rat. The faun was himself again.

"Potent stuff this, mm'm a liddle jumpy. That was some rat."

"You white as chalk." Smith turned around. "Somebody you saw?"

"No, I'm not used to this hard stuff," she said. "My sensory system is playing tricks."

"Right, let's get you home; Friendship Heights, huh?"

He brought her back in her convertible with the top down, the wrong top she thought. Caroline knew she must work harder for this man. In her driveway, as the courteous agent walked over to open her door, she watched the van across the street. He caught her look and almost jumped out of his skin when the van swayed slightly on its suspension.

"There's somebody in there," he whispered harshly.

"Of course, there is. This is Tenley."

"What's that supposed to mean?"

"My mistake," she shot back, irritated by his roughness, "you'd have no problem in the back seat of a Porsche."

It was a grim joke and a regrettable one. He was a good-looking man, just not tall. He did not have to put up with this.

"Big house you got here," he said, holding firm, but nettled.

"Everything is relative."

"You full of crap," he said in the same good-natured tone.

What amazed her was this new need to test her attraction by throwing things at it; to see if it withstood the impact. It was a destructive method, as all great things were born weak.

"May I be frank with you?"

"You doing okay."

"You don't deserve this."

"Is there a sweet girl underneath?"

On the porch, the sneakers did wonders. She was about to tell him how he could find out, when he changed the subject.

"I seem to recall an autopsy row over the cause of your late husband's cancer. What was that all about?"

"The opinions of the experts were inconclusive," she replied.

"I hate that phrase."

"The tumor was associated with radiation. We use weak radioactive materials, but you'd have to set aside all safety measures for a long time to cause that level of damage. Our insurers stood to lose money and found an expert who called it their way."

"There is always an expert waiting to be of service."

"Robert and I were two of a kind, always talking cellular mutations."

"That's way above my head."

"I miss Venice, the canals, unh oh boy.."

"Never been to Europe."

Caroline found the sexual tension unbearable. She put her hands on him for the first time.

"Let me take you there tonight."

It took no more than that. They tumbled into the empty house in a happy hilarious state because they had touched that way. She couldn't help this new drive. And when he relented, he came to her in a frantic tumble, a carnal contact so brutal she could barely remove her dress. The pearls from Robert held out for the duration. Her white old lingerie did not. Neither of them dared to hold back to allow the slow movements to catch up. Slow movements are for survivors, not for lovers that meet once in a lifetime, mindlessly and without protection. With pink pajamas on the floor.

Afterwards in the bedroom she lay looking at a smiling man in a silver frame and couldn't remember his arms.

"You screwed the old man good," she murmured to her dazed faun, as she drifted into sleep. The garbled words made him smile.

Strolling about the house, Smith pondered inhospitable books. He eyed scribbled formulas on her desk without a modicum of understanding. He recalled interviews with her colleagues, flipping through the reports, the tales of unbending scholarly austerity. He could only commiserate about the pathological row that erupted over her husband's cause of death. Whatever was amiss, she was the innocent bystander.

He had never been this sexually in stride with a woman before. It was almost scary. In the kitchen, by the toaster, he read the Post article again.

Here he found a girl he understood; an easy-going woman in love with her kid; the determined daughter of an old-fashioned father. After reading it twice, he picked up her silk pajamas and put them up against the glow of her skin, watching her sleep in the bedroom.

She smelled of goodness. What could a woman like that have to do with the evil of Alexander Rykov? His breed would not make inroads with her for all the money in the world. Smith felt primitive fulfillment, but he knew that their passion was unfit for the drudgery of morning. It gutted his essence. He was caught like a salmon, ready to be reeled in.

He was a small catch, he knew, but he would not race the slack in the hope of getting off the hook. He would let it run its course and suffer the ultimate cruelty, to be thrown back into the pond.

Out on her porch he stood and smelled the roses that grew wild in her garden. He studied the van across the street. The red-white-and-blue diplomatic plates were common in these parts.

"Back seat of a Porsche, huh?"

He called the Old Mansion to run the plates. Turned out that the vehicle was used to transport diplomatic mail for the Russian Embassy. Their interest worried him. She must not testify about the Georgetown hit. Were they involved? Had they bugged her house? What happened between them could land him in deep shit. He needed a way to protect her sterling reputation. The fact that Caroline had stated that she saw nothing of value when Rykov was murdered was a silver lining. There would be no need to use his sexual transgression to damage the credibility of a witness.

"Need your help, partner."

Special agent William Parker Jr. hid his surprise at the other end. This was the first time Smith called him at home, first time he called him partner and first time he asked for his help, and here it was, all in one sentence.

"I want it unofficial," said Smith. It had to be something.

Almost an hour later, a bunch of loud drunkards passed by Caroline's house in an old open Buick, foul mouthing the world at large and Tenleytown in particular.

"Yo man, I gots to piss a barrel," a black dude yelled and threw an empty beer can in the street, then loudly declared his need to piss on the entire neighborhood.

"Sho wanna juice up this cocksuckin white-ass ghetto." The old Buick wheezed to a stop by the curb in front of the black van.

Smith sat in the shadows of the porch watching three big dudes get out of the car. One pushed back the Uzi slung across his shoulder and proceeded to piss in the bushes. The others used the side of the van and the pavement. The rest argued loudly as they jostled recklessly around. They were not the kind of guys you ask politely to go away unless you are very cool, or if you are the U.S Army. Finally, as the bunch had argued off enough steam to climb back into the car, they drove off to the sound of obscenities shouted at the houses along the road.

Moments later, a Chrysler crept up the drive. Smith went to join his newly declared partner in the street. They didn't have long to wait. With vandals in the heartland, the bomb squad was quick off the mark.

"Hi there, Mark," Smith greeted the squad officer, an old buddy of his. "Look, captain, I got a witness in protective custody and a van abandoned in front of her house. Probably nothing but it makes me nervous. Check it out for me, will you."

"Wrong place if you want to damage the house," Mark shone his flashlight at the back, then walked up front. The van had no license plates either way. His men studied the undercarriage with mirrors and Mark tested the locked doors.

"Want us to tow it?"

"Don't like it. Union Station got me nervous. Let's have a look."

The cops unholstered, as Smith withdrew the small sledgehammer brought by Junior and with one swift blow smashed the curbside window. As flashlights lit the insides of the van, Junior held up his camera, picking up a panicky man in the back. The front door opened. Another guy stepped out. The one in the back tried to cover the window with a coat. The cops yanked it out. "You can't do this," bellowed a man in thick accent, opening the front door. "This is diplomatic vehicle. You have no jurisdiction."

The metro cops moved on him in unison, unimpressed by an asshole claiming diplomatic immunity. They spun him around and slammed him against the hood, then dragged the other cat out. The cops who had seen the surveillance equipment in the back were taking no nonsense. The car had no license plates.

"These Russkies spying, Carl?" asked the captain.

"Let's check their papers. If they are diplomats, the Russians must be scraping the barrel."

On first inspection, their papers seemed in order, but papers could be forged. Smith insisted on checking with the Russian Embassy, providing the Bureau with an engine block number to check. It all took time and while it went down, Junior busied himself in back of the van with a camera and oversized pockets. Eventually, the doubts were dispelled. The duty officer at the Russian Embassy confirmed that the driver was attending a private party in Tenley. The van was indeed a diplomatic vehicle. Protests on the breach of diplomatic immunity were brushed aside. Driving without plates was a federal offense. To prove the point, the police were glad to write out a ticket that would never be paid.

Smith was left to ponder the consequences as he watched the two unlikely diplomats climb into their unplated vehicle and drive off in the direction of Embassy Row under heavy police escort. Junior had picked the van clean of evidence, but this was highly advanced surveillance. They had already streamed their encrypted booty into the wrong hands. The only silver lining he could hope for was that whatever the Russians had picked up tonight would never be accepted in court.

CHAPTER 9

WHILE THIS WENT down in Tenley, a tall man stood alone in the dark, off the park, watching the black waters of the Anacostia River. The lights by this stretch of the river had been put out. Broken glass felt like crunchy pebbles underfoot. Listening, staring into the middle distance, he heard the launch before he saw her. The sound rose above the soft gulping of the waves. He spotted her by the soft secondary illumination; the eerie light retained by the pool of humid pollution that hung over the city. She was a small U.S Navy launch, doing the heave ho in the choppy backwash from the riverbank. She had two men on board, a petty officer, and a sailor at the tiller.

They took the mainstream downriver, doing it the Washington way, passing the decommissioned destroyer USS Barry. The tall passenger knew they'd soon be entering the broader Potomac and hated the thought. The launch was unsteady enough as it were.

"You must change clothes, sir," the petty officer said curtly and handed him a neatly folded pile. It was a navy uniform, complete with underwear and socks.

"And your shoes," he added, indicating with his foot a new pair of black shoes. His seaman's leg moved in harmony with every movement under the boat. Without a word, the tall man took the stack of clothes, put the bundle down aft in front of the helmsman and sat down. He was feeling the first flutters of seasickness.

"Here?" he asked, the word disfigured by a thick Russian accent. The petty officer turned to hand over a duffel bag marked U. S. Navy.

"Yes, sir, right now. Put your clothes in the bag; all of them, and your sidearm. We board a navy frigate in ten minutes. Once on board, you will immediately be taken to your quarters. You are not to speak to anyone. Do you understand, sir? Not one word!"

The passenger nodded. It was a valid point. Out in the deepening darkness of the Anacostia River, he started to undress, pushing his secured and holstered Heckler into the waterproof bag along with his clothes, one garment after the other. Finally, naked, healthy, and well-built was not how he felt with the Anacostia undercurrent taking its toll. He rose to sift through the neat stack for a new pair of boxer shorts.

"Your watch, sir," said the petty officer.

"Watch," the tall man retorted angrily, "what about watch?"

"I'm sure our Admiral can afford a Rolex, sir, but you are not our Admiral," said the petty officer. "Put the watch with your clothes. It will be returned to you."

Reluctantly the tall man shook his head and did as he was told. He pushed the Rolex to the bottom of the duffel bag, next to the gun and pulled the strings. Making a knot, he handed the bag back to the petty officer who received it in perfect balance. He looked the tall man over in the fading light from the tainted halo that hung over the capital. His body was almost perfect.

The petty officer put down the duffel bag carefully. In a fluid move, he pulled a blue-steel Walther automatic from under his dark blue navy windbreaker, moving its weight in an easy arc to within an inch from the smooth skin on the tall man's muscular chest.

The barrel had a silencer.

The petty officer smiled sadly as he pulled the trigger twice in rapid succession.

Two bullets for Boky Voronin.

CHAPTER 10

THE HEADLINE DID not ease her hangover. The Post scoop was predictably focused on human interest. A world-famous researcher who doubled as a Washington socialite got caught in the crossfire outside a Georgetown kindergarten. They had turned her into the all-American hero who waded through a hail of bullets to protect her child while Aleksei Ivanovich Rykov, the alleged head of the Russian Mafia, was gunned down in the heart of the capital. The police confirmed that the old man's five-year-old daughter Krupskaya was among the casualties.

The Post had firsthand information from several sources that this was a suspected dispute over drugs. The Russian Mafia had used Afghan contacts to elbow in on the West Coast market and fighting over spoils lead to this gangland murder. No surprises. The police were searching for a Russian thug named Boky Voronin that left the scene after the drive-by shooting.

Not bad, thought Caroline dimly; transformed without any effort of her own from well-known to world famous in a single day. Her daughter Mary had been brought to Georgetown Hospital with minor injuries. The police were stonewalling and kept her under heavy guard. The Post could confirm through unofficial channels that Dr. Glyn-Griffith was the only witness to the Georgetown killings. She had emerged unscathed, but the authorities feared for her safety. A tight-lipped Justice Department played down her importance in solving the murder, pointing out that this was a drive-by shooting and there was an all-points bulletin out for the suspected assassin, Boky Voronin.

Caroline put down the paper and grimaced. After another Bloody Mary, her head was clearing up. Old Rykov's presence in her thoughts was no longer as disturbing. A pot of coffee and she returned to the Post. It was neat. Kuznetsov could have written this for her eyes only. Last night, her faun had told her that the Russian who led the attack contacted the Post and asked them to arrange a deal with the FBI, claiming that a female witness could back his version of the killings. With Dr. Glyn-Griffith's identity revealed, the Post felt free to release it. Caroline threw down the newspaper and decided to visit Mary before dropping in at work.

She found Mary pouting because they had to scrap a planned visit to the Air and Space Museum and a mule drawn barge ride from Georgetown. Neither was suitable with an injured leg. She promised Mary to drop in at the *Cheshire Cat* to buy books they could read together in bed at home. She would arrange a week off from work, and there would be no books on malignant cells for a while; a happening in itself. She left Mary with a promise of returning in the late afternoon to take her home.

After a call from the police, she had to take a detour. Caroline found Patrick Miller behind a small untidy desk in the lieutenant's cramped quarters in a downtown office. The thick cigar suffocating in his heaped ashtray, laced the air with acrid smoke that stopped her in the doorway. Breathing would make her sick in minutes. She knocked and watched Miller lift his feet from a stack of files on a crammed desk. He swiveled the chair and lowered stained stockings to the floor, one more smell to the brew.

"Just the person I need; been trying to reach you, Professor."

"I guessed as much," she told him and drew another breath from the corridor, as Miller stashed the half dead cigar between mischievous lips. The man was clearly in high spirits.

"Fished a John Doe out of the Anacostia River this morning, off the Navy Yards; unidentified white male."

"That would be Boky, the bodyguard."

"You sure got a head on you, girl. You bet! Reckon he's the snitch who phoned the Post. Your call, Professor; you the witness. Guy's having a reunion with his boss downstairs. Guess nobody warned him about going public."

The thought of Ivanovich waiting for her in cold storage was profoundly disturbing. His evil influence last night had started to fade. The night with Smith had done her good. Caroline followed Miller down the stairs, oddly pleased the traitor Boky got his comeuppance, her thoughts still running on parallel tracks.

"Is this Boky, Mrs. Glyn-Griffith?"

Caroline shivered in the cool air.

"Yes, Boky Voronin." Shaved for the occasion, she thought.

"You sure about this?" Miller nodded at the middle-aged pathologist in moss green scrubs waiting to cover the well-tended face.

"Positive!" she smiled amused, they had him water combed Voronin.

Miller grinned. "Funny people the Russians; I met army big-shot of theirs at an Embassy party. You know, this a cultivated guy. He wanted to see the great American play; To Kill a Fuckingbird."

"It is a novel," she said with an involuntary grin.

"See what I'm saying, one-track minds, the Russians." Miller actually winked at her. "Mighty fine of them to spare us the trouble. Was a clean job. Guys don't want pigeons singing to the Fibbies. Shot twice through the heart."

"May I see Mr. Rykov?"

He looked at her curiously, chewing his dead cigar. He was having a hard time figuring what this shapely piece of ass and the old exterminator had in common. Caroline suspected he had heard about the events of last night, that the lady was tramp.

"Sure, why not."

The masked pathologist slid Boky away and pulled out another slab, another terminated life filed away in a drawer. It felt like hers, but it wasn't. A lifetime of excess beyond the boundaries of ordinary men. The pathologist uncovered a stony face, a chest cavity probed for evidence, - flaps of skin draped back in place. Had they found a heart, she wondered. She was revolted by her misgivings, cramped by a curious attraction to his vast corruption and twisted morals. A line was visible through the cropped hair, the skull emptied of its brain. How did she allow this to happen?

Sensing his icy silence, she staggered and cracked. Her escorts caught their breath, as Caroline started to hammer the stocky chest with her fists.

"Take it back you bastard!"

Although used to expressions of runaway grief, this was unexpected. Miller, grinning. The Professor had a connection to the old vermin, and was now happily abusing his corpse.

The moment passed.

Stooped over an indifferent body, Caroline lifts his right hand to look for a blister to match to the one on her finger. Nothing. His words came back to her. "I made experiments, - touch me!"

Out of sight, she squeezes his fingertip hard, - startled when two metal pins slip out of dead tissue, - needle sharp. "Jesus Christ!" Had he uploaded himself, his mind? Was that even conceivable? Deep within, she knew that thousands of brilliant people had died in the decades of her experiments. Women with strong minds were her best targets, although most succumbed to insanity.

Caroline eases the pressure, and the pins withdraw. Takes care to tuck away his arm, fingers down. Raises head with a bewildered look as agent Smith enters the room like a faded memory. His eyes teetered between commiseration and longing. Love would not stand in her way this time. Had he seen her outburst? Caroline averts her eyes, steels her resolve, and turns abruptly to the lieutenant.

"I wish to change my statement from yesterday.

"I reckoned. Did the Russian pervert harass you?"

"Shut up, Miller," Smith snapped.

"Thing is, they were close". Miller made an obscene gesture, "threw us a tantrum to prove it. And you, agent Smith, are you screwing our star witness?"

When Smith failed to reply, the lieutenant's leer widened.

"You Fibbies bother me. No ethics. Mrs. Glyn-Griffith's up to her elbows in this, playing hide-and-seek, fucking with you."

Carl Smith held his tongue.

"Miller's partly right," said Caroline apologetically, "I lost my nerve. The post-traumatic stress disorder causes memory lapses. It became too much to cope with, my child in hospital, and her friend shot. Apparently, my mind lost contact with the incident. Now that I've found it, I want to add to my statement."

"Thing is, case as good as solved. Sure, you can add what you like but you already identified Boky Voronin. We got our man."

Miller turned to take them upstairs. He sat Caroline down in a bare room at a bolted table where she stared at the chipped wood to avoid Smith. His ugly companion, Parker Junior, joined them, standing by the wall, preparing to take notes. The lieutenant turned on a tape and put the mike down in front of her with a long hard glance, chewing on his dead cigar.

"Let's have it then."

She studied the microphone briefly before she spoke, opting for the tone she often used in her lectures.

"I saw Boky the bodyguard kill his partner, Galina. He put a handgun to her head and fired. Galina had her gun out and was about to intercept the man hiding behind the old oak, the man who shot the driver Pavel and murdered the child Krupskaya before he shot old Rykov. You must know by now that two guns were used. It is my duty to come forward to help you put this murderer away."

"Would you be able to identify the second assassin," asked Smith.

"Yes, I saw him kill Rykov, and Babushka, clear as day. He is the man I saw yesterday morning when I dropped Mary off at kindergarten. He had been watching Rykov at the time from behind that same tree."

"Same guy, same morning, same place; reckon you getting your fingers crossed, lass."

"That morning when you saw him, where were you," asked Smith.

"I was behind the wheel on the phone, after Rykov left. I saw this man step out from behind the oak. He was picked up by a gray Cadillac limousine. He had a full head of white hair and wore a gray suit. I would recognize him anywhere."

Parker Junior scribbled furiously. Smith balanced on the edge of his feet; caught doubly in excitement and in fear for a woman he loved more by the hour. He had thought of little else since last night. He couldn't believe his luck.

Patrick Miller was not as easily moved. This wasn't fair play. He did not like what was coming down. This was Father Christmas stealing back his gifts. Not that he held fair play or Father Christmas in higher regard than most things, but this could seriously screw up a case that was already sewn up.

"You talking turkey, lass?" He pulled the wet cigar and spit bits of tobacco. "Gray car I can accept. Gray Caddy's something else. A girl making a car like that plain ain't normal. Might as well give us the license plate," the jeer was for the record.

"It was a diplomatic license plate, red-white-and-blue." She recited the number. The only sense of hesitation was they thought she was joking. Even Miller smiled. It was a sweet moment.

"I have a photographic memory, when it works."

Smith and Parker Junior exchanged glances.

"Give you any odds it's somebody close to him," said Smith.

"How you figure," fumed Miller. "My guess you leaned on this girl in more ways than one last night." Agent Smith didn't take the bait.

"A driver does not leave his armored vehicle unless ordered by a superior. Somebody with authority must have ordered him out of the limo before the shooting started. Taking him out was the signal. The driver was not in on it."

Caroline eyed Miller, pleased with her agent. Wasn't he a clever dick? Parker Junior left the room.

"This a drug hit guys, lots of gravy. So, if Boky had an accomplice, it changes nothing." It was Miller deciding to go with the flow.

"Let's shake the tree and see what falls out," said Smith.

"You can shake all you want," said Caroline, "the expendables fall out, probably on your head. You think you are dealing with common criminals. That is a problem. They are power brokers with legitimate shares of the loot and turfs to protect. When the master pulls, the marionettes dance. Come to think of it, Carl, you are dancing, and I can see the strings."

"Power brokers killing kids," he said, irritated by her lecture.

"Nobody holds power without using it, agent Smith," said Caroline. "If you don't play the circuit, your power goes flat. You can't even keep your car battery charged without using it."

"Now, there's something to remember, sonny." Miller was watching Caroline with a renewed spark of interest.

It took Junior less than a minute to trace the vehicle. It belonged to the Russian Embassy. This specific limo was not in the open pool. The car was used by Vasily Aleksandrovich Kuznetsov, a former KGB general and his private staff. Kuznetsov was the ranking military attaché, apparently with interesting extracurricular activities. As the head of Rykov's security, he was a perfect contender. Junior strode back into the interrogation room with Kuznetsov's file and placed it in front of her.

Caroline nodded. "That is the man who murdered Babushka," she said, "the man who shot Mr. Rykov and the driver Pavel."

"For the record," injected agent Smith, "Dr. Caroline Griffith has identified Vasily Aleksandrovich Kuznetsov, military attaché at the Russian Embassy as the murderer of three Russian citizens on American soil."

Miller spat out the involuntary end of his mangled cigar and took some time to relight the shoddy thing. It could be said that it gave off such a disgusting smell that his breath became bearable. He glared first at Smith, then at Caroline.

"I have a sworn statement. You saw nothing. I don't think you were lying the first time. Exactly when did your memory return,

Mrs. Griffith, before or after you slept with agent Carl Smith of the FBI."

William Parker Jr. bolted upright.

"My memory was back when I woke up this morning."

"That would be after you slept with agent Smith."

"That is correct."

Smith straightened more slowly. Why couldn't she avoid the complication by pointing out that it was none of his business? Did the Lieutenant have a private line to the Russian Embassy? Miller was a frequent guest at Carter's, but that was an official meeting.

"Every dog has his day," said Miller in quiet amazement. He knew he had landed the big one when Smith too let the allegation slide. Miller shook his head slowly at Parker who was waiting for his partner's refusal, the slave cursing his master, his black dong aching after his whore. The woman was a catch. You had to admire the bastard. Miller cleared his throat.

"Thing is, Mrs. Glyn-Griffith, this is the most unethical investigation I've seen in years. Smear campaign more like it. Don't get me wrong. You got a great story. Back in the red-baiting days, reckon you could dine out on a story like that for years. Who was it sold you on this crap?"

Caroline sat watching a black giant assessing damage, silently cursing Smith who was too far gone to care. His love was true. She knew it by his gratitude last night. That was important. Not for the sex, but when he realized that she too was true. Well, that part of her anyway.

She stood up calmly.

"I am prepared to pick out this murderer from a lineup, if that is what you need, to testify in open court. You know where to reach me."

"Where you people come from?" Miller turned off the tape recorder. "This is Washington. The guy you fingered is an accredited Russian dipshit. You Fibbies fart in his direction and he's back in Moscow."

"This is a Bureau case, Miller," said agent Smith, sounding none too sure, "diplomats, foreign nationals, organized crime. Our turf, and Caroline needs protection. I'm not letting you out of my sight."

"I don't want your protection," she snapped, shying from the truth.

Patrick Miller plucked the tape from the machine. He grinned when both agents rounded on him.

"Evidence gathered by the metropolitan police, guys. I'm hanging on to that."

"This is federal evidence," said Smith, "we need a copy," he tapped his breast pocket, "don't tamper with it, Miller, I taped it."

"I'll send a copy to your director," said Miller, "Moffett is leaving. Figure he won't be part of no cover-up in his last days in office."

Caroline felt relieved enough to laugh at the lot of them.

"Gentlemen, I have a kid waiting for me in Georgetown Hospital. I'm taking a leave from my lab for a week. There are arrangements to make. Would any of you know the names of some good children's books?"

They were still thinking when she walked out. Smith wanted to give her a good-bye smile, but the smile didn't surface. It was cornered by his suspicions. He turned to Miller.

"Only the three of us know of this interview."

"Sure, if you count jungle-boy here but he's so ugly nobody would believe him."

"Look, Miller, be serious. Kuznetsov is a KGB general gone legit. He knows his way around. I want us downwind from him."

"Sure, he's into big deals with our military," Miller shook his head, "plugged into the networks. I heard about some big trade-off in the works between the Russians and our government, in the billions. Dude got more contacts within the beltway than we got streets and like enough, he paved them all with gold. When the military get rolling, you don't want to stand in the way. I figured that out myself, and I'm not even smart."

"I want this under wraps, Miller, while we arrange protection. We cannot hide her. Her work is too specific for any of our programs."

Miller pondered this oblique angle, spinning like a cat. "Yesterday was her protection. This broad won't give up her job just because you ask her. She was safe with a drive-by shooting and you let her mess it up." Miller turned to square up to Junior. "I think

Long-dong-black here's aching to screw your fair lady. He thinks he knows how to handle a white woman of quality."

Smith shook his head slowly, unable to stop Miller from rambling.

"Hell, we can't all live blamelessly. I'm starved for a piece of ass almost every day but risking her life like that, agent Smith, giving up your career for a one-night stand. Was she that good?"

Half an hour later, Miller walked to his Mercedes 350 cabriolet in the center of the police parking lot. He put the key in the ignition and turned up the music, punching his cell phone.

"How ya doin', general. Yeah, it's the silly season, that's the gospel truth. Sure, she made your John Doe. Pinned Galina on him for good measure. Thing is the pigeon pulled a switcheroo. Saw you casing the kindergarten earlier that morning; saw you kill the old geezer and his kid."

Miller listened to the general's angry voice.

"That's right, promised to sing her head off." He moved the receiver from his ear at the angry voice. "Yes, sir, it's slipping away. Saw you gun them down and gave us your license plates; a photographic memory she tells us. Thing is, if that sweet thing's lying, don't tell that to an American jury when defending a commie KGB general. You up against the American people here. You the nigger they caught raping the Sunday school teacher. Not a good place to be."

As he listened, Miller scanned the parking lot. The heat was building up to a swelter.

"Sure, it's a setup. Whoever is after your hide is leaning on her. About that deal of yours, someone's out to wreck it. Don't know how they want to work it. Good news, I got agent Smith by the balls for fucking the witness. Professor admitted to it on tape, so you don't need the surveillance from last night. No American court would touch that one anyway."

Miller frowned and brushed the sweat from his forehead. This was his ace in the hole, his bonus.

"Sure, I can solve your problem, but I figure it puts me in the line of fire. I'd prefer to solve it some other way. It can get messy, and it will cost."

Miller listened through the music. He leaned against his Mercedes and stroked his abdomen. Miller found it firm as ever. The human mind has a habit of holding on to old impressions that are long overdue for a review. He glared ruefully at the asphalt.

"Don't threaten me, you commie jerk," he offered kindly, "your money don't cover suicide. I go after her, they come down on me. Never prove it, but they'll have my pension. Smith and his jungle-boy are already spreading the word."

Patrick Miller rose slowly from the warm hood of his navy-blue Mercedes and studied the gleaming mustard ox hide. His forehead glistened like pearly butter. He spoke sharply into the small cell phone, this time in a horse but controlled whisper.

"Let me understand this correctly, general. You are offering me two million to cut this short?"

The lieutenant cast his eye around the sun-drenched parking lot, a man sensing entrapment, then opened the door and eased onto creaking upholstery.

"Sure, we in business, today my offshore account. There's only one way to make the professor understand. Her kid. As I said, it can get ugly. Won't lift a finger till the transfer is confirmed. You got to clean up afterwards for both our protection. The Fibbies won't take it lying down."

CHAPTER 11

T THE LAB, a few miles to the south, Caroline fought
boredom as she waited on Dr. Taylor while he buttered up
a nobody on the phone. Closing her eyes to the view from
his office, she pined for more robust times. She was getting used
to his private thoughts crowding hers. She recalled lying naked on
the vast terrace to the Pitsunda Datja, looking over the Black Sea.
Pleasant memory, swimming in the tiled pool with four girls and
two fine boys. Six of the best, coming up for recommendations to
the Bolshoi, well aware that his acceptance opened doors to the best
tutors in the world, and a grueling training schedule. Here they
were glad to give him a more worldly performance. They tiptoed
around him, naked and slender, gracefully looking for ways to
please; waiting to serve the nation.

These kids hunted the datjas by the thousands, too many for
a man who had the private use of hundred great state buildings.
Feeling their hands on him, he felt nothing stir, so he let them please
one another. He was always on the lookout for promising candidates
for more important state services than ballet. His eyes roamed to the
Black Sea. Pitsunda was built by Krutchev, a man of simple needs.
He never grasped the loneliness of total fulfillment, the point you
reach when you have nobody left to bend to your will, except the
few who'd rather break than bend.

Caroline opened her eyes to a mediocre Washington office, listening to a nobody utter deferential goodbyes. Bill put the phone down and stared at Caroline without hostility.

"You won't believe this. That was one of the most powerful men in Congress, Senator Greenbaum, praising my work."

"And asking about me?"

"Said you were well acquainted since way back, but he kept calling you Dr. Glyn-Griffith; asked how you were holding up, was there anyone else in your life."

"Wanted to know the weak spots, did he?"

"Why is this influential man asking questions about your private affairs, Caroline?"

"Intriguing, isn't it?"

"Senator Greenbaum wants to know all about our program. He is chairing a hearing on foreign policy and didn't have time to set up a meeting now, but he offered to use his influence on our behalf. He praised our work."

"Except your name did not appear in the Post."

"You cannot hide the truth from the ranking Democrat on the Senate Intelligence Committee. He is very cozy with the community. His aides would have prepared him. He asked if I could meet him at a state dinner tomorrow if he wangled an invitation. I haven't a clue what this is about."

"Don't worry; a perfect PAC man is always willing to serve the nation. Have there been other offers?"

"I thought it was our cancer breakthrough."

"Why would they care about that, Bill?"

"Some colonel called to invite me down to Florida. The army has a research center tucked away down there near Pensacola, a small outfit, he said, couple of hundred people. They are hunting for new talent; they'd fly me down. Said there would be time for a round of golf afterwards. Seemed like overkill to me."

"Trust the army to make the brass-knuckle approach."

"I asked some friends, but they had no idea. Way above their heads."

"Anyone else?"

"Dan Rayburn, the industrial magnate, called me in person to offer a season ticket to the Redskins games; never talked to the man. He wanted to know all about you. Said he met you the other day at the Lehman's junket. Said you ran out on him. And here I was thinking you didn't mingle?"

"It was his girlfriend who had me walking on coals. She was way too attractive. You have seen Marie Luise von Ettersberg on television. I wanted her for myself. I suppose you know the feeling," she smiled at his tanned undistinguished face with fun in her eyes, watching his jaw drop.

"I can think of a thousand ways to have fun with that splendid animal. Did you know she studied ballet? She was on the shortlist for the Bolshoi. Guess somebody found she had more valuable qualities."

"However much I love to chat, Bill, I have a luncheon appointment in ten minutes. I'll drop by again before I pick up Mary, to give you my schedule if there is something important. I need a few weeks off."

Several hours had gone by when Caroline returned. It was unlike her.

"And you displayed your usual assertiveness?"

Dr. Alice questioned her wryly as she checked the cross-references to use in Caroline's planned absence. She knew that in any argument that did not entail scientific significance, her boss would patently refuse to stand up to a quivering jellyfish.

"Told him a few facts of life, did you?"

"I will Alice, if you accept to be in charge while I'm gone. You can call in whatever help you need. Don't worry about the cost."

"I'm impressed," said Alice with an unimpressed smile that turned into a frown when she saw Dr. Taylor walk into the adjoining lab, probably to find out if Caroline had returned from lunch.

"I am also commandeering his new assistant. I think you better take her under your wing."

"Bill won't agree." Had her boss taken a stand? Alice sighed in a brief moment of doubt. It was unlikely. She lowered her clipboard to watch Dr. Taylor pass his new assistant in the glassed-in next lab, bending to give her a pointer. Resting a hand on her shoulder, he did some light massage, aware they were watching. Alice's moment of doubt passed. She raised her clipboard.

"Has he made a move on this kid yet," Caroline asked.

"Not yet, breathing down her neck. She doesn't like it but she's single and squirting hormones and here's this man dangling a permanent job in front of her with proper pay and long hours."

"Waiting to dangle something shorter in front of her."

"He knows what he's doing. She's great enough flirt to stray into his trap."

On the other side of the glass, the assistant was about to cut open her first rat. Her demeanor made it obvious, she wasn't up to the task she was hired to do. Bill would be promising to help out later. Leila didn't seem too pleased at the prospect. She put down the knife, looking between him and the rat.

"Thank you, Doctor Taylor," she said doubtfully.

The nominal head of research patted her on the shoulder and strolled into the inner laboratory where he propped himself up on the table in front of Alice and Caroline, the image of a casual professional. He had come to pick a fight.

"You realize that by taking time off, you are risking months of hard work," was his first shot across her bow. "We may need an outsider to fill your position. I think I'll have a quiet talk with Dr. Jeremy."

Alice made her ridicule known by a shrill burst of disgust followed up by an amazed shake of her head.

"No joke, Dr. Christian. Our program is dependent on government funds. We must hire a new head of research who is both an eminent figure and well-connected."

"You sycophantic little shit." Alice's exasperation jarred with the coolness of Dr. Taylor, and Caroline seemed disinclined to respond. "You are on a free ride here. All our results are built on her work, her intuition."

"I'll stick this on the cooler," said Caroline and walked out into the adjoining lab where she tacked up her instructions, passing Leila who sat helplessly fidgeting with a dead rat. The rat was belly up, all pink and pretty. Caroline bent down to help her.

"The first step, honey, is imagination. Let me show you." She pointed through the glass at a suave tanned scientist. Bill was half perked up on a table in the adjoining room, his trousers stretched across an unseemly spot. He was blissfully watching Alice's angry mouth.

"See his crotch? Does that bulge remind you of anything?" The young assistant looked over with an embarrassed frown.

"Bill got one of these up his trousers."

The girl laughed uncertainly.

"The two are inseparable, so eventually, you'll have to deal with his rodent. Look at this beauty here."

Without gloves, she positioned the rat.

"Ten to one it looks like Bill's. Keep it firmly in hand. Then slice like this." With one expert move, she opened the rat from the neck down with a swift movement of the blade. "Pluck out the tumor and voila."

Dr. William Taylor watched his young quarry through the glass as Caroline came back to join them. She had probably been slandering him, as Leila seemed to have caught an uncontrollable bout of cough. Bill tried to sharpen his cold fury into an effort to impose his will on his team.

"You might consider including Alice in your plans, Caroline; she is becoming increasingly difficult to work with."

"I don't have to take this shit," proclaimed Alice and threw down her clipboard.

"I am quitting."

Caroline put out a loving hand to stop her. The deliberate loving touch on her bare neck seemed to paralyze Alice.

"No-good running from a man, dearest, they are everywhere. Even your Fallopian tubes are named after a man. As for you Bill, I just had a private lunch with Dr. Jeremy at the Hay Adams, would you believe. He's as much at home there as at Le Lion d'Or. No wonder money is scarce around here. You are right of course; this place won't remain a peaceful setting with you and Alice at each other's throats. Dr. Jeremy agreed it would be for the best to separate you."

"You went to Dr. Jeremy behind my back?" Dr. Taylor stuttered in a voice he couldn't format into cold fury.

"I took steps to ease you out, Bill. It is nothing personal and not behind your back, it's the Washington way. You have two weeks to pack the pictures."

Dr. William Taylor looked like he had swallowed a tornado and contained it. He was livid. The aspiring politician in him was trying to gauge the effect on his future career. He had staked his future on this platform. It would take years to build another.

"I don't believe this," he said weakly.

"The old boy's network won't help you. Dr. Jeremy is well aware who brings home the bacon. The first rule of your freeloader's union is to know whose work gets them grants to screw assistants in Four Seasons Hotels."

"Hahhh," said Alice.

"You can't do this. I worked my ass off for you."

"Yes, but you are not my maker."

"I never claimed to be. I kept us afloat all last year."

"Yes, you did well by me. I'm not hanging you out to dry."

"Good, this practical joke was in bad taste."

"I talked to a couple of influential men today about you. You want to stay here?"

"There's a lot to do."

"I have a plum deal worked out for you, Bill, a dream position, less than half a mile away, at the National Institutes of Health. You get to do what you do best. Wine and dine distinguished guests and screw the staff. Make the right alliances, talk to the press every day. Make loads of friends. It comes with appointments to high-powered committees and even access to the administration. The pay is double. It is not science, but I don't think you'll miss that. The job is yours if you want it. If you don't, you are out of here anyway."

Dr. Taylor was watching her intently, mouth slightly open.

"Take it on a tender, Bill. What I demand from you is personal loyalty; loyalty to me. I want you there for a reason. The time may come that you think you no longer need me, me being a minor player. Don't make that mistake. We can talk when I get back. I'm not removing my hand from you. Until then, you treat Dr. Alice with proper respect."

Caroline stepped up to her friend and kissed her slowly on the mouth. It seemed an overwhelming urge to fall for; probably Rykov doing the song and dance. Dr. Taylor's hand went to his head to steady it. Caroline let go and sailed out without a word, leaving Alice behind in a stupid daze.

Walking past Leila in the outer lab, Caroline spotted a row of four rats neatly stretched out, open from the neck down. She touched her assistant tenderly on the shoulder.

"It's all about motivation, honey."

CHAPTER 12

OUT IN THE lobby, the angry old man looked into her eyes through the mirrored glass and shook his head with hers. His dark doubts sent Caroline running towards the car park. The drive downtown was slow with the car idling in heavy traffic. In panic, she dialed Mary's room, but her concern proved unfounded.

"Me and Babushka are watching TV."

"Would you do something for me? Would you call out and ask that kind police officer outside your door to talk to me."

"I can't."

"Why not?"

"I don't know his name."

"Why don't you call him Mr. Policeman." She listened hard and heard her daughter call out, twice. There was no answer.

"He can't hear me."

"Then go to the door, open it and call him. This is important. He must be out there, in the hallway."

"I mustn't walk, mom. Eric said so."

"Eric?"

"My doctor. You know him. He is from Culpeper."

"This time, you must walk. You can. Do as I say."

Mary slid awkwardly from the bed to the floor and hobbled over to the door, pulling it open to peep out.

"Mr. Policeman," Caroline heard a thin voice weighed down by space and distance, met only by sanitized silence. Long before she could shuffle her way back to the bed, her mother knew why the white impersonal hallway lay empty and quiet.

"There's nobody, mommy."

The traffic was moving again. Caroline saw an opening and the car lurched forward to weave through the looser traffic, swerving abruptly to avert collisions. The screaming tires didn't catch up with her brain.

"Mary! Mary! Listen to me! Get out of your room. Go into the room next to yours, hear me; the room next to yours. Hide there on the floor, under the bed, until I come and get you."

"Why mom?"

"Just do it!"

"Can I take Babushka with me."

"Yes, she's there for you. Do this for me, Mary, right now, and don't talk to anyone. I'll be there to pick you up in ten minutes."

Other motorists held back, angry but careful of their cars. Weaving down Wisconsin Avenue, she spilled the contents of her purse on the seat and picked the pile for Smith's card, and for once the FBI linkup worked.

"You assured me the police are guarding her room, there's nobody."

"You sure about that?"

"What kind of a dumb question is that?"

"Right, if it makes you feel better, get Mary out of that room. Take her up to the next floor and wait there while I check into it."

"I am not there. I called Mary. I'm in my car at the Nebraska intersection on Wisconsin and the traffic's murder. I'm taking the 35th down, be there in two minutes but there's nobody there."

"Caroline, be careful. My guess; a visit to the toilet. This is a call of nature, simple as that. Call me when you get there."

"Man, and his nature," she muttered.

A few minutes later she came to a screaming stop in front of Georgetown Hospital, jumped out and abandoned her car with the door open. She was wearing a dark striped jacket and a matching straight skirt, a smart twinset that suited her, which was not true of the way she ran in high heels. Almost at the entrance, she noticed a police chopper come in for a landing on the roof. Did they do that here? She didn't think so. In cold hysteria, she rushed into an on opening elevator with several visitors, and more waiting to pile in.

"Take the next," she shouted, barring entrance, punching the fourth-floor button with her body shielding the panel. "This is an emergency!"

There were five with her as the elevator started to climb. A dignified white-haired gentleman made a timid stab at a lower button. Caroline struck his hand away in violent fury.

"Don't do that," she said evenly.

"What," the old man stammered aghast, "are you out of your mind?" He made another uncertain stab without luck.

"Touch that and I'll tear your eyes out and take them with me." Her level voice carried such conviction that it stunned the group. She stared them down, one after the other. None batted an eyelid for the rest of the haul. As she sprinted along the empty hallway to Mary's room, she saw a double action door to a stairwell rock gently on its hinges. Somebody had gone through moments earlier.

Mary was not in her room, but what made her heart sink was the rag doll on the floor. It was Babushka. Caroline flung her weight into the stairwell and listened, just in time to hear a door slam. It echoed with a metal sound from higher up and cut off the tail end of a thin cry. The madness brought her sprinting up the stairs to the roof. The law said that no Washington building could be higher than the statue of Freedom on top of the Capitol. Thank God for small mercies.

Caroline threw open the metal door. She caught glimpse of a small foot, flanked by two men in hospital uniforms, before a police officer shut the door to the already hovering police chopper and backed away in the downstream from its rotors.

Caroline screamed in sheer desperation; her desperate lament cut to shreds by the whining blades.

The officer turned and saw her, turned again, but couldn't call back the chopper as the pilot, banking away, had other things on his mind. Looking to see if she was alone, Miller seized her by the arm. She did not resist him.

"Should've told us you coming! You told the Fibbies she gone?"

"Only that the guard was gone," there was no point in fighting.

"Shucks, lady, you a pain in the ass. I'd sure like to give you some of that back. I'd throw you over the wall, except for them peeping Toms."

"What?"

"Them top executives with brass telescopes," he said grinning as he manhandled her down a flight of steps to the top floor. She didn't grasp what was coming, stumbling into an empty hallway as he pinned her against a steel-clad door. Looking around, he pulled a switchblade from his back pocket. She was saved as a cluster of doctors and nurses came cascading out of a doorway down the hallway. The group came jostling towards them.

"That's just great." Miller tucked away the knife. "You value your daughter's life; you keep your trap shut."

Her head fell in tears against a steel door. The footfalls in the hall faded as she raised her eyes to a reflection, the apparition in the steel. The words came unsought to her mind.

'Are you going to sacrifice our daughter, Caroline? The FBI cannot save anybody. The administration has a hidden agenda. Let me help you.'

The young woman was clearly in distress. The team of doctors slowed to look into it.

"Everything all right?"

"No." Miller replied with all the weight of his rough office.

"Everything is not right. Woman lost her daughter. Give her a little privacy, will you."

Sympathetic smiles and the team moved on. When they were gone, the hallway lay silent. Caroline knew with blinding clarity that too many witnesses had seen them together.

"Get in there."

He thrust her through a steel-sheathed door into an antechamber of sorts with ceramic tiles. It had a single desk by the wall to the left. Miller lit the lamp on it. There was not a sound. The wall to the right supported extended washbasins, also of steel, topped by mirrors. The foyer opened into a private room, dark without windows. Miller spun her around, unable to resist touching her up, pushing her against the basins, her back against him.

"Guess I got to trust you now." He pushed her hard against the edge of steel, waiting for the pain to hit home, enough for her to moan softly. She gave way and put her forehead against the mirror.

"Reckon you can forget the chopper when you tell the Feds that your kid is gone. If Smith does not believe you, she's gone forever."

"I'll do anything to get her back," she whimpered, "only don't hurt her."

"Thing is Professor, I got Internal Affairs on my back because of you. Implicating me won't save the kid. My story will hold up better than yours. If you don't behave, bad things will happen to your lovely lass."

He released his grasp, leaning against her, a large hand on the nape of her neck, pushing her head against the mirror. In panic she realized the truth of it, looking at her pitiful reflection, the tearful features of the old mask, collecting itself. Slowly her anguish faded, her hands became steady. The mask gave an imperceptible smile in the mirror.

"Listen to me, lieutenant. I will tell agent Smith that I don't trust his Bureau, that I am hiding Mary with friends where nobody can get to her. I found the police officer gone but you know he went for a pee, right? Nobody can prevent me from removing my own daughter?"

Patrick Miller thought about this for a while, fitting her contours to his own.

"You got a head on your shoulders. Go ahead, tell him that. Thing is, there's this other guy you accused of murder. Aiming to do something about that?"

"It was a dream."

"You dreamed it?"

"People do that Lieutenant. The dream confused me. The Bureau won't have a case."

"And the plates?"

"I saw that man arrive at an embassy dinner, years ago. What can I say, I have a photographic memory," she murmured and moved her back against him, she did not have to move by much to know that Miller was aroused, "I'll do anything to get my daughter back".

I figure great thinkers give great head. How about that?"

"Do what you want with me." Her voice pleaded and all the time she was looking with a half-smile into the mirror at the old man who smiled so dreadfully back.

"That's a mother's lot; you a mother, you've been fucked." He locked the steel-sheathed door from inside and withdrew his hand to jam his fist up her skirt, forcibly ripping cotton. She saw the old man's eyes widen in panic. It passed. The mask forced a smile.

"In there," he scouted the dark adjoining room as he pushed her into darkness, fishing for a condom in his pocket. He bit off the wrapper and cut her off when she tried to play sexy.

"Spare me the playacting, professor," riding her despair was easy.

"Here, let me," she whispered as he leaned back against a high examination table. He held her shoulder with a strong grip for safety as she pulled the zipper and released his organ in the dark. There was no way she was getting out of this.

"Whoa," came a murmur, "you got some hard-on boy," putting him at ease with a husky tone of wonder.

"Yeah, what you want with agent Smith, anyway? I want to describe to him every move you make, when we compare you at Carter's."

She fingered him expertly and pushed him groaning up on the steady table.

"Reckon Carl's jungle boy is white with envy," he chuckled.

"Huh?"

"Agent Parker, the black mutant. I saw him look at you."

"Lieutenant; your organ reminds me of the bollards they used to secure tobacco boats on the Potomac when I was kid."

Miller gave way against her assertiveness. He lay back and left her to the task. She actually believed that he was the one who had her daughter stashed away. Being this hard two days in a row was rare. First that fringe hospital benefit yesterday and now this.

"You got a big mouth on you, girl. Use it," he said.

It was a necessary concession. Without hesitation, Caroline did his bidding. The Lieutenant was hung like a horse. She was in no doubt that he made love like a horse. With her hands all over him, she worked him as she tugged at his clothes to grunts of his satisfaction, she worked uneasily on the side to put the broad light Velcro straps in position. It was essential to get them where they could be secured in moments if the opportunity arose. In the dark, he'd think they were clothing.

Caroline raised her head from him abruptly to climb up on the table to mount him. It would give her the leeway that she needed.

"You want a tighter spot," she mumbled as she moved above him into position of her final degradation. She used the jostling and awkward climb to conceal her locking of the Velcro straps. She had seconds to maneuver but it was enough. The Lieutenant relaxed in the dark. He held all the aces. The Professor was dead keen on saving her kid.

"Reckon you ready for a real man," he wheezed.

He did not realize what was happening when she jumped to the floor and pulled the last straps into place as hard as possible. She reached her hand in the air and flicked on the blue-tinged operating light above the table.

"What the hell?"

The lieutenant laughed but didn't struggle. This was too ridiculous. They were in a small specialized operating theater. The woman yanked another Velcro strap tight across his arms. He raised his head to gaze at his erection. She followed his gaze. If he was worried, it would be the first thing to go. The Lieutenant was not worried. He tested soft Velcro straps with his arm. It would take a few seconds. The doubt grew on him.

"How long you figure this will hold me?"

She gave him a smile, cold as the clique lights, but kept him calm by fondling him. Then she yanked his gun from the holster and held it for a moment to his warm temple. His skin had started to sweat under the brilliant lights. Thinking better of the empty threat, she placed it on the utensil table to the side. Miller felt like he was on a roller coaster ride when she fished the knife out of his pocket.

"Shucks," he said as the cold blade pushed against his balls, "what you go and do that for?" The woman was not thinking straight. Nothing had changed. He still had the kid, sort of.

"Don't go losing your erection, lieutenant. You wished for a tighter spot. You will get your wish. Let's see what I can do." She put the knife by the gun. Miller closed his eyes. This was pure thrill. He could learn to like this. But as he turned a blind eye, she reached to open a gas throttle marked N2O and slammed a mask down hard on his face. His eyes flew open. Miller started to struggle wildly to get loose, holding his breath, trying to resist the gas.

"Easy," she giggled as she threw her shoulder across his right arm and chest, trying to stall him. "It's laughing gas, to cheer you up." She tried desperately to hold the mask to his face. He got his left hand half free and grappled with her right, striking it aside. With his organs screaming for air, he had started to breathe heavily. His left hand reached her face and started to push, once, twice and she took a pounding on the shoulder. Slowly by brutal body weight, he thwarted her. He was moments from loosening the straps when strength deserted him.

Moments later, wearing latex gloves, Caroline stepped out into the hallway to get a fire ax from its glass cage, returning as Miller came groggily awake. After studying the labels in a small medicine cabinet, she picked the mask from the floor and set it aside, then plunged a needle under his tongue. Again, his eyes ripped open, and the sluggish body stiffened.

"Local anesthetic," she explained. "Don't want you talking dirty. They won't find a trace of it."

The dazed lieutenant sputtered but could not talk straight. Caroline removed his wallet to go through with latex covered fingers; nothing! She replaced it and removed a cellular phone clipped to his leather belt. She studied the menu, flipping through the numbers on its memory card. Most were of legitimate police interest but not all. She cleared those from the memory and replaced the phone.

"You have a lazy mind, Lieutenant, keeping safe numbers to a cellular phone. Aleksandrovich is using Sergei Kurginyan. Even a Ukrainian poet wouldn't tell a pathetic security risk like you where he keeps Mary. You have nothing to give me."

Briefly she loosened the Velcro straps to roll him on his side. Still groggy, Miller pawed with his hand at the table as she strapped him down in a new position. A faraway look came over her face as her fingers felt along the top of his back.

"Just a little pressure on the spinal cord right here, between the cervical vertebrae and you won't feel a thing."

She placed the blade of the small fire ax across his spine and picked up a stainless hammer from the side table. She did not pull up his shirt. Showing emotion, Miller rolled his eyes and made muddled sounds. He was wriggling more effectively now.

"Paralyze you from the neck down for life," she whispered to his sweating brow, watching his pupils widen. She steadied the clean ax blade across his vertebrae. "I know it sounds awful, but I need you quiet and drug free until I can find you a perfect death." She lifted the surprisingly heavy steel hammer and struck the thick end of the gleaming red fire ax once with a precisely controlled blow. The wriggling stopped.

"There," she told him sweetly.

The lieutenant made panic-stricken sounds with a tongue that kept coming in the way, his face was a terrified question mark. The fire ax had sunk a fraction of an inch through the skin between the vertebrae. Caroline yanked it out and put it carefully to one side. Blood seeped out from the slit into the blue shirt. Putting a thick bandage pad to it, she undid the Velcro straps and rolled Miller on his back. She shook her head at his open fly and slack genitals, zipped him up and padded his crotch, lifting his right arm and dropping it. They both watched the hand roll off the table to dangle.

"Bet you've never been this relaxed on a date before," she said.

Having done her cleaning up, there was nobody in the top floor hallway when she wheeled out a patient to position a roller bed alongside the stone parapet of the central staircase. She lowered the side rail.

"Perfect, don't you think?"

The pensive male patient reacted with a manic stare.

"No science can give you back your strength, Miller. Do you want to live like this?"

The patient mumbled something unintelligible.

"If you do, raise your right hand."

More frantic mumbles but no movement.

She pulled a pretty face and stood at his side, leaning over the stone parapet to look down. She saw a large hat cross the marble floor far below.

"The trick," the nurse told her patient, "is to land on your feet."

She rolled him gently onto his side to remove the bloody pad of bandage and then pushed firmly until Miller tipped over the rail and disappeared beyond the parapet. She swiped the air once with the heavily blood-soaked bandage. It left drops of blood on the floor and the stone. Moments later, from below, there issued a distant thud.

The nurse wheeled the empty bed back into the private operating theater to the sounds of far-off commotion.

CHAPTER 13

A FEW MINUTES later, the descending elevator opened with a soft bell and Dr. Caroline Glyn-Griffith walked into a downstairs lobby humming with the excited flurry of activity. She was brought to an abrupt stop, facing a wall of FBI agents. Smith stared at her along with the rest. Had they called her hand so quickly? She braced for their accusations.

Then it dawned on her, they were waiting for the elevator. His men would be on the stairs. It had just been a close call.

With a terse expression, Smith moved to intercept her, to lead her away while his flock filed past her into the elevator. She liked his warm concern. She liked it more than the aloofness of her own heart. That her daughter's abduction troubled him in a tender personal way was a good sign. From the corner of her eye, she saw a man in green scrubs pick at a blood-spattered heap in the middle of the floor while agents cordoned off the area. Smith hugged her gently.

"Is Mary in her room," he asked.

"Who is that on the floor?"

"It's not Mary," he said, grasping the implication.

"They kidnapped Mary," she said tonelessly.

"Oh, my God," he hugged her again in a desperately comforting way. For a moment she enjoyed a lover's embrace to which she must not submit, then pushed him away.

"What happened," he asked in resignation.

"Mary was not in her room. Miller, the metro detective asked me to contact the desk to see if they moved Mary. He said he heard a chopper, so he went up to check the roof."

"Patrick Miller?"

"Yes, I better check with the desk."

"The hospital didn't move Mary. We have that confirmed. The officer on guard duty got a message. He was called off. The message was not from the police. My men are combing the upper floors. You wait here with me."

"They got Mary," she said.

"Sorry, looks that way."

"Miller heard a chopper. Maybe he stopped them," she repeated.

"Miller's dead. That's him over there."

"They killed a police officer," her voice was plain and without color, "if they get away with that, what happens to Mary?"

He leaned his face to a striped shoulder and held her. "They won't get away with it. Miller tried to fight them off. They threw him over the railing. We'll get Mary back. I promise!"

In high heels, Caroline was again the taller one, searching a face that was dear to her.

"You are a good man, but the FBI cannot save my daughter," she smelled his hair, "the government has a greater good that justifies any outcome. You are not in the loop. This is not your fault."

"Bullshit," he hugged her, sensing her receptiveness, "justice is the only issue here, nothing else."

Her features settled without expression and her speech slowed.

"I cannot be frivolous with my trust, Carl. You are blindsided. You have no pull. Our leaders are not evil, but they have a massive deal in the works to buy uranium from Russia. It's a big disarmament issue. And as you said, Vasily Kuznetsov is their ranking military attaché. Me accusing him is a problem for the government. My daughter will not be safe until the problem is solved. What happens to Mary after that is anybody's guess."

"There is nothing you can do. These guys have contacts all over. Let us protect you." He shook her shoulders gently as she broke from him.

"Are you in love with me?"

"Jesus," he pleaded, "yes, if that's what it takes."

"Then don't yank my chain."

She reached to touch his chin in a gentle gesture.

"Cancer must be dealt with cleanly. You cut it out or you die. Rats are my specialty."

"Caroline, please."

"Stay the hell off my back," she told him softly.

Smith looked at her go, sailing to the main door and out into the city on high heels in a straight skirt. Parker Junior walked up. He had been watching them, wearing the kind of smile you wore when somebody falls off a chair in a public place. His boss was making a fool of himself.

Together they stood and watched her go; one smaller guy and his big ugly companion.

"Damn," said Smith quietly, "she's going to get killed."

"But she sure can walk, man," said Parker Junior, "know what I'm saying. I think Miller was right; looking at that back makes my dong ache."

"Can't be much of an ache then," Smith turned to the heap on the floor, "was it a police chopper?"

"Yeah, incoming with a woman in labor, we're checking the flight plans. Broke all the rules; got no business landing here."

"Can we question the woman?"

"No, the doctors won't let us near her. As far as the hospital knows, the chopper left empty. We tracked down the medics. The pilot claims to know nothing but he'll lose his license. For what it's worth, these guys have lots of strings to pull and money to spend."

"I want that bird impounded, dusted for Mary's prints. Have them vacuum it. Get hair references from her room. My guess is there were extra passengers on that flight. I want their descriptions on my desk tonight.

"Anything else?"

"Is the team in place?"

"Yes, Sir, all we could round up on a short notice."

"How many?"

"Seven cars and five bikers."

'How many agents, Junior?"

"Sixty agents, sir, and that is putting a strain on the Union Station investigation. You better have a good reason for this. There is talk. This better not be personal."

"Just don't let Dr. Glyn-Griffith slip away."

CHAPTER 14

S HE LEFT GEORGETOWN University Hospital clutching at the idea of visiting St. John's Episcopal, but her heart was not in it. She had found peace in that church after Robert died. She took a turn down M Street and got stuck in a gridlock on Connecticut Avenue. The fraying tempers and bleeping horns helped her reject the impulse to burden St. John with more of her madness. She submitted to the old man's guidance; not a tear would be shed until Mary was safe. Referring the matter to a higher order was like casting dice for a child's life.

Behind her, to the right, in a Capitol cab, the eye of a man was idly drawn towards her car. He had an oddly shaped head. She recalled the buddy of the Hoyas hunk at Carter's. There would be more of them, and she had to make sure. She checked her watch. Strangely, the thought of leaving her car in the middle of the avenue for the police to tow, did not bother her one bit. She opened the door for air, seized a handful from the heap she spilled from her bag earlier and slipped from her car, ducking to win time.

In the horrendous midday traffic of central Washington, Caroline abandoned her convertible in the street to duck into the metro station at Farragut North. As she glanced from the curb, she spotted four unlikely antagonists shouting across her Saab. Probably the tip of the spear. Two of them took up open pursuit. Standard practice, she thought, sprinting into the bowels of the Metro. They could no longer afford to give her a false sense of security until the others had her covered.

Somehow, the thought cheered her.

She ran down the steps as fast as her condition allowed, timing it right, making the platform well ahead of them. They were still on the stairs when the train rumbled out of Farragut North, destination Tenleytown.

The two agents stared into the dark hole that swallowed their target. One started to pick up the litter, a receipt, an eyeliner brush, a library card. A lipstick had rolled over the edge onto sooty gravel. Caroline had fought her way to the train and spilled from her purse in the panic. The agents walked up the stairs. There was no emergency. The woman was running home.

She never boarded the train. Racing the empty platform to another exit, Caroline could not spot a single agent. With trains every six minutes, it was easy to trip them up. During the afternoon rush hour, she used her inherent tradecraft to ride the system, popping into stores, shuttling into Diamond Cabs wearing a new raincoat; out of Capitol Cabs to blend with the guided flow of tourist. Between cab rides she rode the Metro for good measure. She did it because of the deliberate embrace Smith had offered, not for love, but for expediency. If he was any good, he would surely have tagged her. The Metro was their blind spot. He would not have the staff to cover all the entrances. Whatever happened, she would hang on to her striped jacket.

At Dupont Circle, a rental limousine service picked up a woman who had specified shaded windows. The chauffeur dropped her at the Smithsonian. Getting off, she told him to drive nonstop around the city for an hour while she visited the museum. She asked him to avoid traffic jams and stay on the move. She made a show of writing down the mileage on his meter to keep him to it. Her tip for the deviousness was large enough to brighten his day. He needed no explanation of the clandestine nature of her meeting. He had seen all sorts. It was warm so she left her striped jacket on the backseat.

Boarding the Smithsonian Metro, she changed trains at L'Enfant Plaza and got off at the Pentagon City Metro station where Rykov kept a private courtesy suite at the Ritz-Carlton, using a fingered *nom de guerre*, known only to him.

The suite that was unknown to Vasily Aleksandrovich had a magnificent view of the monuments across the river. Kuznetsov would have liked it, she thought. That Ukrainian peasant had a soft spot for silk coverings, and the decorations in Williamsburg blue were his taste, as was the Chippendale furniture. The thing that Vasily would not like here were the contents of a private safe where several files bore his name. The green safe was in pristine condition. If tampered with, a self-contained burn bag had an independent oxygen supply. The exhaust would turn the paint bubbly from the inside heat, nothing else.

Caroline turned on the copier and started with the procurement copies. It felt good to be back in control. She withdrew two videocassettes and photographs and selected a handful from the stack, already in a fine mood, then sat to write her private letter in longhand to Senator Greenbaum.

Dear Friend

Thanks for your kind words at the Lehman residence. It has come to my attention that a mutual acquaintance, a retired KGB general, has been skimming off funds from the sales of laser-based technology to the United States Air Force. These copies will prove his participation through a thicket of joint companies with Dan Rayburn. Would you be so kind to convince Dan that it would be in his interest to accuse Kuznetsov of defrauding the government? I have also turned over a videotape that came into my hands to Timothy Udall, chair of the Research and Development Subcommittee on the House Arms Committee. I am told there is a second tape in which you reach a private understanding with Kuznetsov. Timothy Udall is laying out the framework for cost regulations for the new Stealth generation. He could use the boost of a small scandal like this. If you are willing to back his proposals when they come before the House Arms Committee, I'm sure Udall would go easy on an influential senator. Take my advice. If the second tape were to surface, it would be as part of a government sting. Give my love to Marie Luise.

Caroline Glyn-Griffith

Caroline took one last look at the photos. They showed Senator Greenbaum in his special ballet tights, trying on all of Marie Louise's many attributes. That girl was something else. The Senator's friend, Dan Rayburn whose trophy he was enjoying is the photos would not be pleased. The vast earnings might mitigate his reaction.

She had a messenger service pick up the two bulky letters at the desk for personal delivery, then called Tsvetayeva, alias Marie Luise von Ettersberg to secure delivery of the letter into the right hands. Using Rykov's codes of clearance, Tsvetayeva was butter in her hands, and she found herself missing that.

Caroline called the cruising limo to pick her up at Arlington Cemetery, two subway stations down, pleased to reclaim her striped jacket. She paid the driver roundly in cash from the Carlton-Ritz safe. Hinting adultery, she cautioned him to keep mum.

It was late afternoon when a young woman in a Burberry raincoat crossed the wet street amid the quaint flophouses in an unfamiliar part of town. Satisfied that her stalkers had not yet picked up her signal among the motley afternoon crowd, she entered a respectable apartment hotel across the street. The Primacy Hotel with its quaint lobby was an old respectable establishment.

"One moment, please, Miss. Are you a visitor?"

The desk clerk who mounted the challenge was a gangly college kid with a big Adam's apple and pimples, doing his studies behind the desk.

"I am a guest in private suit 47. I know the door code."

The young man's Adam's apple bobbed twice, and his face flushed as he looked into the hotel register.

"I need a written authorization or identification," he said, overriding his inherent servility. "I know it's stupid, but management is incredibly strict about this."

Caroline walked over and handed him her driver's license. He was young. Watching him write, an idea skittered across her mind. She had so often found it pleasant to use sexually overcharged college kids for lovers. The involuntary idea rose into her consciousness like a bubble in water, like breaking wind in the bathtub, the burst releasing its rotten core.

Her level sensual stare embarrassed the young man as he wrote in the ledger "Dr. Caroline Griffith visitor in suit 47". Nothing is more daunting for a desk clerk than a socialite scorned.

"Security reasons, ro-rou-routine, thank you."

Embarrassed, silently cursing his stammer, the boy tried to hand back the license. His hand hovered uncertainly between them. The woman did not reach out to take it.

"You are new here. Have you read the security file?"

"Yes, madam."

"All of it?"

"Yes madam," he was almost pleading now, the license heavier by the second. She snapped the card and turned to walk towards the elevator.

"Bitch," the boy grumbled, wiping a trickle of sweat from his brow.

In the hallway on the fourth floor, Caroline punched in the code without thinking. By now, she knew better. To focus led to mental conflict and memory would elude her. It was easier to act on impulse and let it ride.

Memories were a burden. Memories of days with Mary at the Cheetah Conservation Area or with Richard in any capacity were now complicated by an ingeniously administered dose of radiation. The sound of sliding bolts brought her back to reality.

Entering a small mahogany-paneled apartment, she draped her beige raincoat on a chair and surveyed the room. She knew it and she didn't. From behind the curtain, she stood for a moment and watched the patched street in both directions. Once upon a time, this stretch of dingy flophouses had been handsomely renovated with a generous investment of bad taste and money.

"They are late", she murmured, scrutinizing the occasional pedestrian passing on the pavement. On the corner, a leather clad figure in a crash helmet on a nondescript bike was looking up and down the street. The biker seemed lost. She stepped away from the window. By the corner cabinet in the kitchenette, she opened a small hidden combination safe and removed a handgun and phone with a scrambler device. She slid in a battery from the charger and punched the buttons.

"The Primacy Hotel."

It was the pimpled desk clerk from downstairs who answered in a more carefree mood.

"Good afternoon, sir. This is the FBI, special agent Monroe speaking." Caroline selected the same cheerful tone.

"Yes?" The young man was all attention.

"No reason to alarm your guests, but we have a bomb scare in your area. We are asking people to be on guard about unattended luggage, you know the drill. We'd appreciate if you let the police know if you notice anything suspicious. Anything at all. Thank you."

The desk clerk stared at the dead phone. He leaned over the white counter to look along the floor. The woman in suite 47 was a stranger off the street. Did she chose the apartment number at random to get into the building? She had brought no baggage.

On the fourth floor, Caroline picked up the old unsecured phone on the sitting room table. As she did, a red light flashed on the switchboard in front of the clerk downstairs. It came on above the taped marker which said, 'Red light file'.

"What now," muttered the clerk, getting nowhere in his studies of eighteenth-century English literature.

Using the quaint old phone, Caroline dialed. Kuznetsov answered without giving a name. 'A lion's mane, and coward's voice', she thought.

"Good afternoon, Vasily Aleksandrovich."

"Who is this?"

"In return for my daughter, I will inform the FBI that my account of your involvement was a mistake. I staged Mary's abduction myself. I sent her to a colleague for safety. Your problems will be gone."

"What about Patrick Miller?"

"Who cares about Miller?"

There was a long silence.

"Since you made up this story to begin with, your testimony remains your private matter, Dr. Glyn-Griffith. I'm sure you will get your daughter back although not from me. As you know I was never at that kindergarten. Is the Bureau listening in? Did they help setting this up? I am pleased that you retracted your lies. Could we meet privately, to clarify the situation?"

"Yes, but not today, tomorrow perhaps?"

"Where and when?"

"Book a meeting with a friend at the State Department, say at fifteen hundred. Sign in at the desk. I can trace you to set up a meeting in the building. This time Aleksandrovich, don't wear a stocking over your head."

As Caroline put down the phone, the red switchboard light went off downstairs. The clerk had picked up a sealed folder from the hotel safe. Above the seal was a taped marker *'Open in case of red light'* and below was a handwritten message that said, *'Return this folder to owner if seal is broken.'* The clerk broke the seal and read the single typewritten page inside, a few lines in capital letters, unsigned.

The young man dialed suite 47 and was relieved when a female voice answered. She was not a burglar.

"Yes, hello miss, this is the desk, downstairs, uh, we met. I'm sorry, you know, about the security thing. Ah, I wondered if I could be of any service, something from the bar; anything?"

"No thank you." The woman hung up.

"Bitch,' he said again because he had seen the flirt in her eye and would have given the world for a guest like that. He dialed the number in the folder. A man answered without giving his name. The voice sounded irritated.

"Good afternoon, this is the Primacy Hotel desk. Seems we have instructions in our safe, ah, well this is awkward. We are instructed to tip you off if the phone in suite 47 is used. Which is, ah, if my offer of services is refused without a Charlie being mentioned?" He cringed at his own words.

"That's correct. Is there someone up there now?"

"Yes, a woman signed in half an hour ago, Dr. Caroline Griffith, and her papers were in order; I mean her driver's license. Is she unauthorized to use the suite? Should I call the police?"

"Not at all. The woman is the wife of our CEO and she's no stickler for security. Thanks for calling us. Keep your trap shut and there's a hundred bucks in it for you."

"Hey, man, any time. What do I do with the folder?"

"One of our boys will come over and pick it up. He will bring your hundred. You have done well, young man."

The student put down the phone and punched the air in joy.

CHAPTER 15

SMITH LISTENED TO the tape for a second time before he slammed down the earphones to bark to his headquarters at large to get the trackers on the line. His mind felt heavier than the concrete FBI bunker on Pennsylvania Avenue. He turned to Parker Junior with a distraught sigh.

"The Primacy Hotel?"

"Snapped it up minutes ago, apartment used by Rykov. We have an old warrant on the phone. Why would she call Kuznetsov? The word is that Kuznetsov took over after Rykov but why would she set up a meeting with him at State?"

"What is she up to, Parker? Is she involved?"

"Do pigs fly? She caught Kuznetsov off guard."

"Nothing we can use there, clever bastard; too vague about holding Mary. What's this about a stocking? She said nothing about that earlier. If he was wearing a stocking, how did she recognize the guy? How did she know his unlisted number? He asked her that. What is she doing in Rykov's apartment? It has a code we couldn't break."

"If he does a deal for Mary, we have nothing."

"Why would he deliver?" Smith was handed a phone.

Down in Anacostia the black leather clad biker stood watching a battered U-Haul pull up to the opposite curb. A man in an overall stepped out from the rear and gave him thumbs up. Beyond the gleaming black visor, it was impossible to tell gender but when the biker spoke into the built-in mike, it was a male voice.

"Could've told us the target was a pro, Smith."

"How's that," asked Smith, distracted when a ball of energy burst into the large room. It was James Wilson paying them a personal visit. Smith turned his face away from the head of the Washington field division to give the tracker his full attention.

"Target gave us hell of a run, used every trick in the book. If you hadn't tagged her, she'd be long gone. Is this a test?"

"No this is not a test."

"Okay, we have a strong signal, not an exact location. Target's around here, working on it."

"Is there a hotel near you called the Primacy?"

The gleaming black visor reflected buildings in dark blue under an overcast sky. It turned slowly and a solid old building moved onto its black mirror. There was a hotel sign up front.

"Affirmative!"

"That's where the target's holed up. We picked up a call minutes ago. Keep on it but stay out of sight. Do not intervene. We know less than we thought."

"What else is new", said the biker after Smith hung up.

"Good to see you, Jim, long time."

Smith greeted his boss circumspectly. Why would James Wilson break off a Caribbean vacation, a man who never lost the opportunity to bitch about his heavy workload?

"Got the postmortem on that bent cop, Carl?"

"Miller, sure; died in the fall. Somebody put a fire ax in his back to help him over the railing. Cut right into the spinal cord. He was better-off dead. Perp put the ax back in place in the cabinet, no prints. They were pros. Almost got away with it. Our guy spotted traces of blood on its blade. And we got a wound to match. Dr. Glyn-Griffith said Miller ran to the roof to check on a chopper. We got seven witnesses who saw him with her on the eighth floor. They say the woman was distraught and Miller stood up for her. He wasn't all bad, I guess."

"This thing's bigger than its parts," Carl. The background check on Caroline, using the Washington Post as cover. Takes balls to impersonate a star reporter and pull it off. We reached Robert Noyes through the L.A. bureau. Turns out he never met the doctor. Any motives?"

"Nah, to chart her personal life I guess, but why? That probe into her finances was professional. The mysteries are piling up. What can I say Jim?"

James Wilson took his reluctant arm and steered him into a small private office.

"The Director wants this solved quickly, son. The uncertainty is getting in the way of a sensitive deal to buy back weapons grade uranium from a former Soviet satellite, tons of the stuff. You can imagine the pressure we are getting from above. This is a high-level crisis."

"Kuznetsov as much as admitted abducting her daughter."

"Don't start chanting the hymns, son. I heard the tape. Unless they trade and we witness it, you got nothing. Listen, this is now an interagency operation. Manafort is rolling out the carpet. The CIA and the NSA have pledged to give us the crown jewels if we ask them, whatever we need."

"That makes me nervous."

"You are using two hundred of our best. More than enough. Prepare a comprehensive review of the case for our new friends."

"If this so important, why don't you take over?"

"Hey, Moffett handed you this bag of shit; suits me fine. I've seen lots of bags you don't want to hold; bags that blow up in your face. I think this is one of them." Meant as a joke, the words were thick with conviction.

"Doctor Glyn-Griffith is a reliable witness. So, there are problems, but we need to protect her and find her daughter. She can help us nail this Russian bastard."

"Ukrainian bastard. Kuznetsov is friendly with most of the leaders of the former Eastern Bloc, an accredited diplomat. He is also the linchpin behind the biggest buyback deal of the century. That deal is coming down as we speak. The government does not want it derailed. Nobody wants this stuff in the hands of terrorists. Get it over with."

Parker Jr. drove Smith to the Primacy Hotel where Smith ordered the team not to interfere. He felt sorry for his boss who had become personally involved. He felt almost sorry for himself because this was not a good career move.

Entering a quaint lobby, Smith flashed his badge at the clerk.

"Special agent Smith, FBI, you have a Dr. Caroline Griffith staying here?"

"Are you the one I called?"

"You made a phone call?"

"Who else," said the youngster, not about to lose out on his windfall, 'the agent I spoke to promised me a hundred if I kept my trap shut. Here's your folder."

Smith received it with a blank face. The file contained a single sheet of paper, unsigned.

"The seal is broken. We must turn it in, said the boy."

Smith pulled a hundred from his wallet while he read and handed over the note.

"She still up there?"

"Yeah, thanks man."

Once out of sight, Smith rushed up the stairs. She had used all the wrong procedures. After her artistry in eluding his trackers, it was a welcome breath of innocence. Bewildered by the seasoned fieldwork that brought her to Kuznetsov, he welcomed this touch of immaturity, but with his goons on the way, she had less choices than a motorway porcupine.

In the hallway of the fourth floor, he opened the door to the staff stairs and listened to light footfall, going down. There was no answer when he knocked on door 47 but the small luxurious suite opened to his hand.

Caroline had eluded him again.

Racing down the staff stairs to a ground floor restaurant, he passed through its kitchen and storage area where a backdoor stood open into an empty side street. Smith squinted against the bright reflection. The tarmac glistened from an earlier shower. There was an old Indian wino sitting in the shadows of a doorway across the street, humming morosely, balmy as the weather. The man nursed a bottle or something in a brown paper bag, and Smith was reasonably sure he was one of his agents. His attention proved ill spent. Someone had come up from behind, and he stiffened as a cold muzzle touched his neck.

"Keep quiet!"

It was Caroline. She was not being cagey. She sounded dead serious. Her voice was even less thankful than last time.

"Listen, Caroline. You are playing a dangerous game. The desk clerk warned Kuznetsov. His goons will be here any minute. He's an arms dealer, KGB general, for Christ's sake, you are in way above your head."

"He's a former KGB general, currently unemployed. I don't think he will show up in person but if he is keen to get me, he must show his hand."

"You set this up? That's madness." His euphoria over her newfound innocence evaporated.

"They are killers with orders to take you out. What happens to Mary when you are gone?"

"He won't let Mary go, ever. She is a loose thread, useful only as long as I stand in his way. I have no alternative. I must find out where he keeps her.?"

"We are looking."

'He has thousands of places, and you can't touch Kuznetsov. I have information he's willing to take a risk for. I'm a thread that can unravel his power, give his adversaries information to weaken his leverage. This is not a case that the FBI can solve. You may have noticed that I know too much."

"My all-American girl."

"Don't bet on it."

She moved the gun muzzle to the small of his back, leaning against him to hide it as a tall youngster in a white spotted coat came up from behind. Smith could smell her hair as the stranger passed into the street with sacks of garbage, spilling lettuce leaves onto the damp.

He did not see the alluring smile that Caroline gave the boy as he stepped past them out the door. He knew he could turn and take the gun from her. Would it upset her if he did? She would never hurt him. For a brief moment he relived their desperate closeness last night. It seemed a lifetime ago.

"How did you find me," she asked at his ear.

"You made your call to Kuznetsov on the hotel phone, an open line. Why? I saw a digital phone up there, with a scrambler; was the battery flat?"

"Is that your first lie to me?"

He grinned at the wet street. "You found the tag. Still true; it was the call that placed you. Where did you learn to lose a tail like that? And be careful with the gun, it's not a toy."

There was a soft slamming of several car doors out in the steamy midday. The dish washer passed on his way back in. The gun lost contact as Smith leaned out to watch, too anxious to notice as Caroline stopped the stranger with a gun to his face and finger at her lip. Did the young man think it was a joke, staring as she backed away with a smile?

Two Mercedes saloons had parked by the curb. Smith, counted as the men crossed the street to enter the hotel up front.

"There are five," he said hoarsely and breathed a sigh of relief as his back bumped into her. "Make a great change if you follow my lead." He looked up and down the balmy street and reached for her hand to pull her out the door, and out of danger.

"Let's go," he said, but the hand felt coarse and heavy. He turned and looked into the inscrutable eyes of a tall buck toothed boy who smiled in his confusion. Caroline was gone.

He flew up the stairs, able to see her above, shouting that the elevator was on its way up. They could both hear it. She ignored him, and when he burst into suite 47 for the second time, he found her standing by the wall looking helpless and scared.

"Jesus, Caroline, my men have orders not to butt in!"

"I'm staying."

It was too late. Groping for his cell phone, he pulled the Beretta as two men walked calmly through the open door. He pushed the button and let go of the phone, looking them over. Two more guys walked in. Their coolness under pressure did not please him. The general was not among them. Unbalanced mentalities were the worst, but these guys were not unbalanced.

"Special agent Smith."

The speaker was casually dressed in expensive threads with an almost undetectable accent, his abrasive features offset by good built and outgoing personality. Two of his goons packed Colt Commanders aimed loosely at the floor. The third he couldn't place, as if it mattered. They were basic tools, short and stubby with all the chuck capacity needed to propel pieces of metal through soft tissue. Not heavy artillery but enough to polish off an agent. He raised his FBI card, a bit dramatically, like a vampire hunter with his cross. The smile of the handsome Russian reached all the way into his engaging eyes.

"We have the hotel surrounded. Put down your weapons. Don't make this worse by resisting."

"I am unarmed," said their well-dressed speaker, "and well informed. There will be no cavalry. We are wearing vests. You must go for the head every time unless you aim to crack some ribs. Do you think you have it in you?"

"Can take you out."

"An unarmed man, agent Smith? They tell me you are a disciplinarian. That is a problem for us. I suggest that you make an exception. Of national importance. For you it can be the beginning of a new life, not the end of an old unremarkable one." The man did not lose his smile. "The offer is that instead of dying, you walk out of here with a million in cash and no strings attached. You will never hear from us again. Your administration will be grateful, although I doubt they will tell you."

It was hopeless. He couldn't shoot an unarmed man, even one with English smooth enough to demand years of KGB training. That left three assassins with their shooters barely raised in his direction. A glance across his shoulder placed Caroline who stood petrified with her back against the wall.

"Sounds tempting," he said, and the hoarse apathy of his strange voice spooked him, "in exchange for what, exactly?"

"You simply point your service piece at the trash behind you and take her out. That is all it takes."

Smith turned around to look at her. In panic, Caroline steadied the wall with her hands behind her. A moment passed. They could have killed him with his back turned, but they didn't. The offer was serious.

"You have killed before, agent Smith. You will be called to testify that you shot Dr. Griffith in self-defense, which is technically true. We leave the gun that killed Galina in the Rykov hit with her. Her prints will be on it. When you asked her if she had assisted

Boky with the Rykov hit, she pulled her gun on you and fired. Being a professor, she missed, and you shot her once through the heart."

"Is that all?" said Smith as he studied the bosom he fondled a lifetime ago. It heaved less than he expected.

"A million in cash is waiting in a car outside. Do this and walk out of here. We need that bit of trust between us."

Smith couldn't feel anything, maybe sadness. He would draw fire before he cleared half a circle. Raising his eyes to hers, he marveled at her blind trust in him. They had offered him a million dollars and she was not afraid. Her eyes said so. The panic in them lay there like a thin sheet of ice over warmer water. You did not want to skate on this ice. It occurred to him that her panic was not to be trusted. His arm dropped slowly.

"Can't do it, soldier." He eyed her mournfully. "I love this piece of trash."

"Put the gun on the floor, slowly, safety catch on."

Tired sick, he turned to place the Beretta on the carpet, questioning his sanity, falling for a woman he had met and made love to within an hour, and barely exchanged a sane word with since.

"Push it over, carefully."

Not a chance. They followed his foot with riveted eyes, sensitive to any last desperate attempt, their Colts leisurely prepared as the talkative Russian pushed the gun out of reach with a well shod foot. Smith knew that their masters, however influential, could ill afford to have his death linked to hers. This hotel was not a place for a final solution. They would take them somewhere else. The trackers would follow. He had told his men not to interfere. He must find a way around that.

Smith never saw Caroline pull the gun.

It materialized from behind her back, a devastating Sig Sauer. With a rock steady eye, she pulled the trigger three times in rapid succession. There was no silencer. The sound was earsplitting. Large slugs sent brains onto walls, corpses tumbling every which way. Each of the three took a hit to the head, a smoking gun aiming firmly at the unsmiling spokesman. The man shifted his gaze from the Sauer to the eye behind it, and found it equally empty of emotion. He could see nothing beyond the fixed mask.

Agent Smith rounded on Caroline in a bewildered state, unable to put her mindless act down to a mother fighting for a child. It was not an image of the woman he loved. The shock proved too great for words as he bent to pick up his gun.

"Leave it," she barked, "down on your belly."

In involuntary recoil, both men started to kneel.

"Not you, Sergei."

"You know my name?"

"There were five of them," Smith protested from his knees.

"Where do you keep my daughter, comrade?"

As she spoke, one of his men stirred. He already had half his face on carpet. Caroline shot him in the head, her gun back on the speaker.

"That would be a dead man talking, Dr. Glyn-Griffith"

"Your word and I wing you for the Feds. Surely you can sell your friends at Langley a secret or two. You were part of my trusted bodyguard for years. The FBI loves to protect people. Give me your answer now or I will put you in my Kiev coffin."

The man stared at her with a sudden broken look.

"How do you know this?" Their eyes met.

"Is it still working; your old zek-sense. I won't ask again. You know who I am. Where do you keep her?"

"This is madness, they should put you away."

"Traitor!" Her malicious voice was punctuated by a fifth shot. The man took a brutal hit to the knee. Hissing and in shock, the spokesman spun to the floor and landed with his well-trained shoulder on agent Smith who stifled a groan as the man rolled off him.

Caroline walked past them to kick guns out of reach, then snatched a pair of handcuffs from the safe and linked them up expertly. Emptying the contents of a small bag onto the desk, she flicked open a leather wallet with magnetic cards. Pocketing them, she watched Smith on his stomach, her gaze drawn to his tight butt. With a distant smile, she reached to pluck the radio emitter from under her collar where he had placed it when he hugged her in the lobby of Georgetown University Hospital. She seemed pleased that neither of them had let love blind them.

The long glistening pin looked ominous.

"Let the FBI take care of this, sweetheart," Smith started to plead from the floor, "you have no idea what you are up against." But his total lack of conviction was unlikely to sway her.

"You are so great at taking charge." She came up from behind him to kick his feet apart. For a moment he thought to trip her up, when with notable force, she plunged the pin deep into his buttock. He felt a sharp stab of pain as it went in and gave a surprisingly timid moan. Smith turned his head and saw his transmitter stand there like a marker on a map.

"Smartass," she told him gently and was gone.

The elevator opened into to the lobby with a bell. The terrified desk clerk followed the woman as she walked up to the desk. She wore a smart raincoat and held a carrier bag from Burberry's on Connecticut Avenue. The heavy set man who hovered across from the clerk covered his gun as she came up. As the woman turned to the clerk, the man looked her over in hostile arrogance.

"I thought I heard shots in the hotel. Is something wrong?"

"Somebody's watching TV," said the stranger with latent aggression in his voice. The woman turned her eyes on him and fixed him with a pointed smile like a fencer wielding a sword. She took in a big frame, crowned by a small head with bushy eyebrows, a chin modeled after a railway cowcatcher and equally pockmarked. The face, centered by a weak red mouth, was not her type. Caroline broke off her careful study and turned to the clerk.

"Are you a visitor? In that case, this young man needs written authorization or identification."

Swallowing, with a bobbing Adam's apple, the clerk shook his head to warn her off.

"Fuck off, lady," said the man and gave the elevator door a concerned look. This wasn't right. As he looked away, the woman offhandedly withdrew a smoothly fashioned slab of steel from her carrier bag. She moved the large gun easily without fanfare. Nothing gave it away until the man felt its presence at his cheekbone, about the same time as she pulled the trigger. His mass tumbled to the floor, committed only to the laws of nature. The woman casually returned the Sig Sauer to her Burberry bag and gave the milk white pimples across the desk the sweetest of smiles.

The boy watched her smile in slow motion, as in a dream. Perfect lips drew into the beginning of a bemused pout, then slowly and deliciously pulled up and back till the pout gave way and her face broke, with baring of teeth. It was the most beautiful smile he had ever witnessed. The perfect teeth parted to allow her cheerful voice to enter his silent dream. They were the same words that he had offered her one hour earlier.

"Security reasons," she said, "ro-rou-routine, thank you."

The clerk stood in trance behind the desk as she sidestepped the pool of blood gathering on the beige carpet. Then she half turned to address him again. The boy felt like a pillar of salt.

"My room is a real mess too," she said.

With that, Dr. Caroline Glyn-Griffith stepped out into the failing afternoon.

CHAPTER 16

G LARING IN DISGUST at the early evening street, Smith stamped the pavement angrily in front of the Old Mansion on Pennsylvania.

"I'm on the carpet and you lost her. This is fucking incredible." He eyed the large black Lincoln warily as it pulled up.

"Stay on it, you ugly bastard." Smith hung up as the door opened and Thomas Moffett, Director of the FBI, leaned over to wave him inside.

He crept into the seat facing Moffett, grimacing as he sat on one buttock without being too obvious, easing a hand back to massage the aching spot.

"I heard she tagged you," his boss gave him the once over from across the aisle. Smith dropped the pretense. It was all over the Bureau.

"Right, you're almost presentable!" The Lincoln moved and the monstrous Old Mansion banked away like a silent spaceship. Moffett pulled an electric shaver from a hidden compartment. "Shave," he ordered.

"Your lady friend bothers me, Smith. Don't like the way she took out those foreign thugs. Not the act of a desperate mother. A trained assassin would be hard put to carry that off. Something else bothers me; in your report, Caroline alludes to a hidden Government agenda, that we will sell her short. Did she mention anything specific?"

"You are saying she's right?"

"Some influential power brokers are asking me about this woman. I am stalling. That's not good enough. There is only one man in Washington who cannot afford questions he cannot answer. And it isn't the president."

"Kuznetsov didn't like to be in the dark either, sir. We are picking him up, are we not?"

"Not yet," Moffett checked his watch with a look through the green tinged windows at the looming White House.

"The stakes are too high, son. Two hours ago, Director Reisman of the National Security Agency informed me that Kuznetsov is about to have dinner with Dan Corwin, their deputy director. We were asked to be discreet; not to harass a guest of the government."

"What is this about, sir?"

"Let's wait until after the F.P.S.G. meeting. I want to see who is involved. Kuznetsov is street-smart with an ugly twist. He knows how to use whatever power he has."

"F.P.S.G., sir?"

"Ad hoc meeting of the Foreign Policy Strategy Group. We will be attending in a few minutes. High-level, so keep your mouth shut. Speak when you are spoken to. And see to it that none of it gets out, ever. They are touchy about whistle-blowers."

"How high-level, sir?"

"The usual gang, Al, the president's chief of staff, Director Manafort from CIA and Director Reisman from NSA, our national security advisor, secretaries of the armed forces, some brass, all branches. You know the setup."

Smith didn't.

"Foreign policy strategy and nobody from State?"

"State wouldn't touch this with a pole, son. I'm called in to straighten out the rope before they hang themselves. I suspect they are cultivating diplomatic back channels to Moscow, bypassing both State and the Russian Embassy. I'm not entirely sure."

"The Bureau involved?"

"Washington's a jungle, Smith. You never know where the next attack comes from. Certainly not with the Iron Triangle cozying up to the Russians. The Bureau has its back covered in case of a public uproar. There is nothing wrong in going after legitimate benefits, but I don't like the way these guys do business. It smells worse than the Iran-contra affair already and the shit hasn't even hit the fan."

"What exactly is the Iron Triangle, sir?"

"You a newcomer in this town, Smith?"

"I try to stay out of politics, sir."

"I didn't know one could," scoffed Moffett, genuinely amused, "I always found Washington within the beltway to be a fishbowl. Do you know what that makes you?"

"A fish inspector, sir?"

The Director gave a reluctant smile while Smith tried to fit a fishbowl into his Washington jungle.

"Fish out of water, son. I like how you handle yourself, but you better wise up. Agents without political backing don't last. The cozy partnership between defense contractors and members of Congress is no secret. Some call it the backbone of our nation. Everybody wants a piece of the bacon."

"Why do you want me at this briefing, sir?"

"I need your background on that darned woman. No time to debrief you. Her life is public. We interviewed hundreds. What we see is a stable profile. What happened today is harder to understand by the minute."

"She was an innocent bystander who witnessed a murder."

"Wish it were that simple," sighed the Director as the car stopped, "we are here." They climbed out of the car.

The meeting was in the West Wing. In Moffett's footsteps, he passed along the White House corridors, tight jawed as a mouse gnawing on a high-voltage wire. No other building impressed him this way. Perhaps it was the absence of size, so unlike the other mastodon buildings of official Washington. He often visited the spacious offices of the Old Executive Building, but the old granite edifice across the lawn always left him cold.

The White House was neat and trim and smelled of power. It was the chip at the heart of a human computer, a place where you pledged your life and found it meaningful. Along hushed corridors, agent Smith massaged the buttock where Caroline plunged the pin. It was a strange way to express love.

They entered a large well-lit room with a warm yellowish glow, high-backed upholstered chairs in leather set around a gleaming hardwood table. There were few of the trappings of power, more like a boardroom meeting. A sidelined presence of a group of air force brass, struck the military note. The Chief of Staff called the gathering to order. Hardly a day passed on the news without the blunt spoken Alexander Downey clearing up some confusion.

"Draw your straws to the stack, gentlemen."

The absence of the Attorney General confirmed his fears. The meeting was not about justice. Bleeding hearts were not welcome. These brokers didn't decide personal matters. Smith turned to sit by the wall, but Moffett took him by the arm and steered him to a chair at the table. He sat down reluctantly.

"I don't have to remind anyone there may be repercussions," the chief of staff looked around the table, "from the death of Aleksei Rykov. Our task is to advise the president on that matter."

In the silence that followed, the CIA director, Jim Manafort, nodded a balding head at an aid. Instantly the lights dimmed, and a large color photo came up on a screen at the end of the table. The snap was taken with a high-powered lens and showed an old man holding the arm of a small girl, walking here in a peculiar fashion, forcing her to walk lopsided. Smith recognized the face. The aid spoke in the clear concise voice for which he was chosen.

"This man, as most of you know, is Aleksei Ivanovich Rykov. Our preliminary results indicate the girl was his daughter. Little is known of this man other than his vast influence. We have few public glimpses into his life, but those that we have are revealing."

A new picture flashed onto the screen.

"In Reykjavik when Gorbatjov brought Reagan within a hair's breadth of selling out our Star Wars program." The aid pointed a red beam at a modest background figure.

"We have identified this man as Rykov. Officially at the time, he was the General Secretary's private doctor and had unquestioned access."

An older photo came on.

"Nixon with Leonid Brezhnev, boar hunting in the Soviet Crimea," the red dot landed on Brezhnev, "Brezhnev was by now a geriatric junky and only technically alive." The red dot moved.

"And here is our man, the keeper of the drugstore key, Brezhnev's official physician at the time."

"Rykov was not a doctor," injected John Manafort, "he advised Yeltsin on astrology."

The CIA Director was fingering the top secret preliminary NID, the blue-striped National Intelligence Daily for next morning. It was unusually thick. So was the smaller, more exclusive, FTPO preliminary beside it, a white cover with the number one. The handful of numbered copies 'For the President Only' on the table was telling. Only twenty people in the world are in the power loop that read this daily intelligence document. Some had to suffer the privilege of doing so in the presence of an armed escort.

"Rykov's many roles were designed to mislead the world about the man and his influence," the aid continued. "Until the breakup of the Soviet Union, they did. Rykov never held public office. Nobody voted for him. Handpicked by Stalin, he became one of the main movers behind GRU and the KGB. He never held any public rank in either organization."

Special agent Carl Smith found himself looking at an old grainy black and white photo of a plainly dressed young man in his early twenties with an arrogant stare.

"The only existing photograph from the early days. This accidental snap of him was taken in Moscow by the wife of a foreign diplomat."

The snap widened to include the two men in the foreground, the real subjects of the photograph.

"Rykov in the background as always, and in the loop as always." The red beam honed in. "The Georgian who headed their secret police, Lavrenti Pavlovich Beria, Stalin's private executioner," the red dot moved, "and Stalin. The two pillars of the old guard and this unknown boy. The rumor is that Beria executed his family when he was a child. It remains a speculation that Rykov, at the age of 25, had a hand in Beria's execution after Stalin's death in 1953. Rykov has no known kin except his daughter, and we only know of her because she perished at his side."

At this point, Al Downey, the chief of staff had had enough, butting in, he gave Director Manafort a scornful look.

"Why can't the CIA or the NSA tell me by what means this man wielded his formidable influence. How is it that old stalwarts like KGB general Kuznetsov cowered in his presence? How could he casually use these men like errand boys? He used Kuznetsov to look after his own security."

"I'm told he was not looking that hard," said Moffett dryly. None of the others cared to comment. The aid continued.

"There are tales of legendary evil, Rykov's intense satisfaction in inflicting torture. Whatever truth there is in these stories, he was a good man to have on your side and a bad one to cross. We worked with him last year on the deal for two tons of weapons grade uranium and he delivered as promised."

The old granular photo was replaced by a color snap of a nuclear container being loaded off a military transport plane. Smith recalled it as the political coup at the moment.

"Rykov agreed to the deal and gave the order. It was carried out to the letter. We paid seven hundred million into his bank account, legally and with full knowledge of the Russian leadership. You don't get that kind of pull from the stray dogs robbing Russia today. The man had vast spheres of influence, and it extended to the rulers of many nations."

Another photo, another man, and Smith recognized the lion's mane of gray hair.

"For months we have been negotiating for more weapons grade uranium. We asked Rykov to help in the matter. He proposed a new deal to limit the spread of nuclear technology. The package was ready for his decision when he was assassinated. Our liaison with him was this man, former KGB general Vasily Aleksandrovich Kuznetsov. He now tells us that Rykov's death will not affect the deal, but it is unclear if Kuznetsov has the authority to act."

A snap of another face, handed out by Smith to selected agents a week earlier, replaced Kuznetsov.

"We have reason to believe that Rykov's chief rival within the organization was general Orlov, whom some of you know personally. We know he arrived in Washington earlier this week on a private flight cleared into National. He went underground and has not been heard from since. For the record, Kuznetsov claims that general Orlov gave him the go-ahead to wrap up the deal before he left the country. We suspect that Orlov was behind the Georgetown hit but we have no proof. We need an urgent decision. Any action on this deal is fraught with danger but taking none is worse. We are told that the uranium is ready for transport. We do not want it going absent without leave. There are multiple willing buyers."

"The only remaining witness to Rykov's assassination is Dr. Caroline Glyn-Griffith, a Washington doctor with impeccable credentials, and a brilliant career in medical research. Many of you have met her."

The aid stopped short when Al Downey boomed out, glaring at the FBI Director.

"My question, Tom. How is the Glyn girl connected with this can of worms?"

Smith watched Thomas Moffett gather his thoughts. His boss would make a good poker player. He had no answer to this question.

Moffett briefly opened and shut a thin folder embossed with the Bureau seal.

"As far as the Bureau can establish, Miss Glyn and Rykov met for the first time early yesterday morning. There was no prior contact between the two and no clear connection. I brought with me special agent Carl Smith," and Moffett paused a tick too long, "who may have a more intimate contact with the Glyn girl."

Smith sensed lingering distaste as dozens of unblinking eyes inspected him; too many to meet. He stared at the table instead.

"This said," Moffett sighed deeply, "another bit of information has come to light. Something that an old, distinguished Washington law firm has brought to my attention."

The FBI Director paused briefly for accent.

"Precisely two hours before his death, Mr. Rykov deposited with this Washington firm his last will and testament." Moffett looked up at faces that slowly lit up with interest.

"In this legally binding document Mr. Rykov stipulates that in the event of his death, all his assets revert to Dr. Caroline Glyn-Griffith to be disposed of as she sees fit. In a separate sealed letter, he asks dear Caroline, as he calls her, to adopt his five-year-old daughter, Krupskaya. He points out that in case of his death; the child has no living relatives on the face of the earth and appeals to her kindness."

"Caroline knew nothing of this."

Smith, who had caught his breath, couldn't bite his tongue fast enough to prevent blurting out. Thomas Moffett turned ever so slightly to eye him, none too amicably. His apprentice had not been spoken to.

"The will is still sealed and so is the accompanying letter."

The Director turned to the silent table.

"A question arises. Why would this cold war dinosaur, this wily power broker on the global scene, hand over a lifetime's worth of blood money. It is curious, is it not. Why hand over his empire to a perfect representative of the American dream he fought against all his life?"

Smith could see the men around the polished table were aroused but had nothing to add. They left the mystery in the hands of the FBI Director, hanging on his words as he continued calmly.

"The Glyn girl is of old Washington stock, raised on a liberal diet of open debate. She married into a respected family of politicians, many now sadly gone, but Rykov would have hated every one of them."

"What are his assets?"

Trust the chief of staff to ask the relevant question. Smith shook his head irritated. Moffett looked worried.

"His accessible funds in the US bank system alone exceed two billion." He made a small nonchalant gesture. "I have a feeling we are looking at the tip of an iceberg, because most of his holdings are abroad, frankly out of reach, not my table really." He looked remotely at Manafort, the CIA Director.

"Would you happen to know what political party Miss Glyn supports?"

The question from a smiling Alexander Downey was directed at agent Smith but went unanswered as Smith did not pick up on it; waiting as he was for his boss to reply.

"Just kidding, son," the chief of staff said as he measured him up. "I forgot the name. Smith, was it?" The snub got his attention. This was a politician who never forgot a name, especially when he had it on paper in front of him.

"It's an easy name to forget, sir."

"So, agent Smith, you are the lucky man who knows our mystery heiress most intimately. What is your impression?"

"Caroline never knew the man. She met him earlier that morning. Thought she was talking to a kind old gentleman who was dropping off his granddaughter."

"Which explains nothing," Al Downey frowned at him as agreeing murmurs went around the table.

"On the contrary, sir, it explains everything."

This they didn't expect. Smith was angry now and a little excited. The news of the will had opened his eyes.

"Caroline was the target of a sophisticated probe into her finances. I suspect Rykov. Our interviews show that her few distant relatives answered questions under the false pretense of being from the Washington Post. The interest was about her relations with family and friends. With an article in the pipeline, nobody suspected foul play. Robert Noyes, their journalist on the story had nothing to do with it. He was in Los Angeles at the time."

He had their attention now, if barely. He took the plunge.

"Rykov was setting her up. He wanted a faultless American identity for his daughter, Krupskaya. He had laid the groundwork. Caroline has few friends or close relatives, for a reason. Her parents were killed in a traffic accident nine months ago. The truck driver was a Ukrainian expatriate who complained of chest pains before the accident. He survived but left the country soon afterwards. Three months later, her husband falls victim to a freak brain tumor caused by radiation that nobody could explain. By the way, his parents died only months later, allegedly of natural causes."

He gave it a moment to sink in.

"Rykov, who has dispatched all her close relatives, has a plan; if he remains unchallenged, he has a simple way to his endgame. He befriends Caroline and her daughter Mary. They would be invited abroad where they would disappear in a way that causes no suspicion. Their two daughters were strikingly similar. Could have been twins. Probably why Caroline was chosen in the first place. A few months abroad at Mary's age, and distant branches of Robert's family would have no reservations about embracing Krupskaya as their own kin. The old man was not only creating a spot free past for his daughter, but a politically eminent past."

Smith guessed that to these men, it was an unlikely scenario, but he found them watching him curiously, half convinced, hardened by brutal Washington infighting. He waded on, "the problem is that his position was under threat. What happens to his plan if his enemies get to him before the pieces fall into place? Rykov spots a masterstroke, a spin on the same motive, an insurance policy in case of his death. He makes Dr. Glyn-Griffith his sole heir. All that research money is a powerful argument. I'm convinced that Miss Glyn would have adopted his daughter. She is a kind person. Krupskaya would become the toast of official Washington. The caterpillar turns into a Monarch butterfly. I need not tell you guys that with all this massive PAC money, she'd have all the high-level contacts Rykov could wish on her. He figured if he could hang on to power, in time he could use that for his own purposes. If not, by putting his will in place, he took care of his daughter from the grave.''

There were nods around the table, appreciative murmurs. Al Downey leaned back in his chair. He continued to glare at Smith as he cranked up the well-trained campaign smile.

"You were wrong, son, Smith will not be an easy name to forget. Good work, Tom. Good work."

John Reisman, Director of the National Security Agency, added a thought. The serious old gentleman had been slowly nodding. "You may be right, Carl, this is how the old man played his hand, with pitiless foresight."

From the corner of his eye, Smith noticed a breathtaking young military woman enter, wearing a tight Air Force uniform. Did they pick these girls in some strange beauty contest, watching her slip the three-star Air Force General a folder and stand back deferentially, watching her man, only her man, alert to his slightest nod. Would he like a shoeshine? She'd lick his shoes. Would he like them buffed?

Would he like anything else buffed? It was a full-blood performance. Smith felt intensely that his only concern was to keep these men from betraying the woman he loved. Time had a way to turn the color of noble blood and shit to the same hue. There was no way to tell the difference. Had any of these guys been burdened by noble intentions.

"Miss Glyn identified Vasily Kuznetsov as his murderer. The old man was assassinated in the heart of our capital."

"Our concern is national security, son," said Al Downey.

Why did everybody call him 'son', he thought, but he was out of line and sensed their dislike. They were about to trade his woman for a corrupt Russian General accused of murder. Again, it was Reisman who rose to the challenge, turning to the FBI Director, not his underling.

"The Glyn girl rescinded her sworn statement. Her tainted testimony will not be admissible in court." His palm lifted slowly as if he was doing something distasteful. "No jury will accept her impartiality after inheriting a fortune from the victim. And gunning down several Russian security agents is not helpful. To the point. Kuznetsov could not have assassinated Rykov. It has come to my attention that during the assassination, a high-ranking public servant sat in a meeting with Kuznetsov."

"That's my jurisdiction," snapped Moffett.

"What the fuck has that got to do with anything," Reisman snapped right back, no longer the serious old gentleman, "the public servant meeting with Kuznetsov was my deputy director."

There was bad blood between these two. Smith was in no doubt that Caroline was considered expendable. He held his tongue.

"Gentlemen," smiled Al Downey. The Chief of Staff was pleased with himself, inhaling the combustible atmosphere.

"Dan Corwin, your deputy director," Moffett asked softly, "the man who, as we speak, is dining with the former general?"

"The same."

"You are offering a former KGB general a false alibi to salvage your uranium buyback scheme? That is why we are here," Moffett sighed.

"We must look to the greater good," the NSA Director said quietly. Why do you say we are offering him an alibi? I trust you're not listening in?" Reisman looked to the head of the table, at Al Downey. The Chief of Staff took the ball and ran with it.

"Are you listening in, Tom?"

Thomas Moffett gave an obscure smile and hesitated long enough to keep them on their toes. "I better come back to you on that," he said doubtfully. The shadows of skeletons past passed through the room. They let them pass in peace. Nobody wished to cross Moffett. After a short silence, Reisman lifted one palm and continued.

"We believe Kuznetsov is acting for General Orlov, Rykov's rival. We cannot hold these men to some moral high ground. We deal with this right here and now, down in the mud." Reisman was on the defensive. "We need to roll up our sleeves and get our hands dirty, in the national interest."

There was silence, but Moffett would not fall in line.

"Al," he spoke slowly to the room at large, "some of us in this administration hold the constitution to be in the national interest. I may choose to fall on my sword over this. I will do so publicly. I take no part in subverting presidential policy. Does the President even know about your tradeoff?"

"Tom, Tom, it's too early for the blame game. You know we can't give you free reins on this one. It is too big."

Now even the Chief of Staff sounded apologetic. It didn't suit him, but he was an expert at smoothing ruffled feathers. Agent Smith watched his transformation and felt his gall rising.

"Sometimes our national policy must steamroll over a problem, to straighten it out. That's what steamrollers do, Tom. They straighten things out. We cannot compare long-term policy to short-term tactics. Kuznetsov has diplomatic immunity. All we can do is to create an incident. We lose the initiative. Protecting their chief negotiator from attacks is no problem unless the press gets wind of it. If there are any leaks, we lose the deal."

The Chief of Staff glared at the others, taking care to leave out the FBI Director. "There will be no leaks," he warned. "A presidential slap on the back is better than his boot in it."

"Tell the Russian bastard to return the child," said Moffett quietly.

Smith felt gratitude towards his boss for standing up to them. The stratagems of these people were lost on him.

"All right, Tom, all right, maybe his men got out of hand. What do I know, but what I'm told? We cannot expect a man of his standing to go around Washington kidnapping children. If you believe these accusations, ask the man to look into it." The Chief of staff turned to frown at Reisman of the CIA as if he was a dog that had left a mess on his desk.

The Air Force Secretary, a mild-mannered bureaucrat tried to grab the attention, but his own brass overrode the feeble attempt, which in all honesty was not unusual.

"Good point," barked a three-star Air Force General, flipping open the folder the young woman had brought, "let's cut the crap, gentlemen. The logistic window is closing. I must get my planes in the air tonight if they are to cross the Urals in time."

Snubbing his figurehead superior came naturally but when the Chief of Staff held up his hand, the General stopped so fast that Smith envisaged skid marks in his boxer shorts. His stunning secretary would clean that too.

"We'll take that in a moment, Frank," Al boomed. "Gentlemen, you have all been of great help. There will be no surprises. And thank you, Tom, as always, well done."

The two FBI men rose to leave while the others remained. Moffett steered his angry young colleague out with a hand firmly on his shoulder. As the door closed behind them, Moffett patted his unruly agent on the back. "You did well son, they are happy in there. I owe you one."

"Thomas," said Smith, unable to bring himself to the breezy familiarity of 'Tom'. "We gave them the green light in there to sell her out. And if you owe me one, I want to question Sergei Kurginyan, the KGB colonel. Caroline could have killed him with the others. There is something we are missing."

"He's being released," said Moffett, glancing at his watch, "we are transferring him to Langley who bought him, lock, stock, and barrel. Sergei is not a man who scares easily but he's out on a limb. My guess is that he accepted a handsome offer. Maybe he's worth our taxpayer's money."

"When do we hand him over?" They were at the entrance.

"Two hours", Moffett told him, entering the Lincoln.

"I need to ask him something."

"What?"

"Something Caroline said to him."

"There's no time. And we can't use it," Moffett said gruffly.

"Caroline told Sergei she would put him in her Kiev coffin. I saw his face. He was shaken. I'd like to know why. As you said, the guy is not easily scared."

The limousine eased through the White House gate.

"All right, ask the man. For all I care, lean on him a little. Convince him that his brothers in arms at Langley won't get to embrace him unless he gives you the right answer. He's not a diplomat. He's a tourist standing in front of a steamroller. Remember, whatever comes down between you, the man walks." Moffett signaled the driver, and the Lincoln drew up to the curb.

"Flag a cab, will you, son. You're on your own. A day is a long time in politics; no getting behind the information curve. Do you know Timothy Udall? A great man; widely liked for his tactical ingenuity. I'm late for his reception. He chairs the R and D Sub on the House Armed Services Committee. I got to touch base with Senator Greenbaum who'll be there; he tipped me off about a serious case of defrauding the government. Said he has hard evidence. That's tomorrow's news, son. The hawks back there won't be happy about that either. I'm not a popular man in this city."

"Will Kuznetsov stay off-limits, sir?"

"It's over, son. Find the Glyn girl. Find her kid if you can. Mop this up. And don't leave too much blood on the floor."

CHAPTER 17

O NE QUESTION? THIS is the agreement?

The handsome Russian, with bandaged and braced leg, eyed Smith warily from the bed, assuming a pale version of his formerly expansive smile.

"That is the agreement. Answer it to my satisfaction and we hand you over to your Langley buddies."

"When can that be, what's the time frame here?"

"When I have what I want. I can release you in ten minutes, if they still want you by then."

"To your satisfaction is a loose term. What does that mean?"

"I must believe you."

"I tell you the truth and you choose not to believe me. I have told you that I know nothing about a kidnapped child."

"What kidnapped child? That is not common knowledge."

"And I know nothing about a general Kuznetsov."

"You came here to see the Lincoln Memorial?"

With Kuznetsov behind the deal, Sergei Kurginyan had every reason not to betray his trust. His boss and the CIA were thick as thieves. A loose word could cost him everything. Smith glanced calmly at his watch but wanted nothing more than to have a go at that wounded leg with a baseball bat. Whatever came down; in forty minutes, he would hand this guy over.

"Fine, agent Smith, what is your question?"

In his mind's eye, Smith recalled the look on this easy face when she asked him. How the impact of her words from one moment to the next shattered his cocky demeanor, turning this unsentimental high-end thug into a scared rabbit in her headlights. And she had not killed him. For some reason she had not killed him.

"Tell me about the Kiev coffin."

Despite his outgoing nature, Sergei was an abrasive man, a trait picked up in a profession where finer feelings get in the way. Suppress them long enough, there comes a time, you won't find them if you call on them. Not so with Sergei Kurginyan. He was deeply shaken. The slow clenching of teeth. Same as before, his features took on a constipated look.

He thought about the question carefully for what must have been a full minute. He was more comfortable with silence than Smith who saw the minutes sweep by on his Citizen watch. He thought about his own people who had bought this Russian mouthpiece for taxpayer's money and were waiting downstairs for delivery.

"This is your question?"

"Provided you give me a solid answer, our paths will never cross again."

"And if I give you a true answer, you promise to hand me over to your Central Intelligence Agency?"

"That is the deal."

"And nothing I say can be used as evidence against me?"

"You are a bloody genius."

"The Kiev coffin," Sergei closed his eyes for another whole minute. When he spoke up, he drew on a well-stocked vocabulary for a KGB colonel. This was an educated thug.

"The Kiev coffin was a method of interrogation used by the provincial Cheka in Kiev during the early revolution. Ivanovich picked it up, that's Mr. Rykov to you, and worked for years to perfect the method. He called it his Kiev coffin. He kept a small cemetery at one of his datjas outside Moscow, the one near Semjonovskoje. Bodies of homeless drunks and tramps found dead in the streets of Moscow were sometimes taken there and buried in a particular way. He had the bodies injected with some special fluid and sealed in thick plastic bags. Mr. Rykov used an eight-man team for this. Eight trusted officers. Nobody else knew what it was about. I witnessed the Kiev coffin only once on a day when his trusted team was a man short. I happened to be the KGB captain posted to his datja at the time."

Suddenly Sergei's face broke into a broad smile. "It was funny, you know. I had barely received my posting when my superiors started to fall over one another to help me out with anything. Men of rank in the KGB cared little for subordinates except to bark at them or beat them up, send them off to Siberia or worse. Suddenly they were offering me, a lowly captain, all the extra food I wanted, any favors, whatever young women I wanted to fuck. I could pick them off the street. These were the best years of my life."

His face hardened slowly, and his teeth clenched.

"Anyway, on this day Mr. Rykov needed me to escort the committee chairman for heavy industry in Krasnoyarsk territory. His name was Mikhail Golovin. He was responsible for the gold refineries and sawmills on the Yenisei River in our central Siberian Republic. I heard later that Golovin had stalled on a mining industry appointment Mr. Rykov had nominated as his own representative. The poor man thought he had the authority to say no. He did, of course, formally. I think he was just another brave man who could not accept the hidden power behind our leaders. I can see him, a kind man of fifty, red cheeks, wavy white hair, a family man, well liked in the territory.

His minister had called him to Moscow to explain himself. He arrived after traveling two thousand miles on the Trans-Siberian Railway. His minister's secretary met him in Moscow and sent him off to the large state datja near Semjonovskoje. Chairman Golovin thought he was to meet his minister. I was sent to pick him up at the local train station in a limousine. I could see he was in high spirits. He had steeled himself against any arguments. He was in his right and he knew it. I will remember him always.

I was instructed not to talk to him. I walked him in silence up to the cemetery. They had dug up two bodies in plastic bags from the mass grave and there was a large coffin waiting. It was open. They emptied one of the two exhumed bodies into it from its bag. There was this incredible stench. They emptied the other body onto a deep coffin lid that lay upside down to the side. The half-decomposed corpses were almost liquid, oozing horrible fluids. I swear that nobody can imagine that stench. Beside the large coffin, there was a freshly dug grave."

Sergei Kurginyan opened his eyes and looked at Smith with the deep accusation of a man forced to dig up what he wished forever buried.

"They made Mikhail undress. The Chairman, of course, protested wildly but they helped him, almost kindly. They treated him like a naughty boy who did not want to go to bed. Four guards, big guys, grabbed hold of him and lifted him naked into the coffin. Two of them pushed him into the oozing corpse that was already there and then the two others tipped the other corpse on top of him. I would say they poured it over him. Then they nailed the lid down."

Sergei Kurginyan swallowed and stopped to compose himself, scowling to fight down the bile rising in his throat.

"You could hear him fighting in there, to get out from under the corpse, only to dig himself deeper into it. He couldn't scream because he would get his mouth full. But he screamed; once or twice. Then they buried him in the fresh grave."

Agent Smith was sweating. This was not what he expected.

"That was the Kiev coffin?"

"Half of it; a few minutes later, they dug Mikhail up. He was still alive. They hosed him down and washed him like a boy, helped put his fine clothes back on. They combed him. They had to help. I think this man was dead inside. I was to take the chairman directly from the cemetery. I can still remember finding Rykov sitting behind his desk in a big airy room, all proper and well-tended while the two of us stood waiting, and I don't know which one of us was paler."

Then he looked up at us and said, "Mikhail Golovin, my captain here and his team made a mistake. My orders were to bury you after explaining yourself, not before. I had them dig you up. I want to hear from you why you did not trust engineer Pavlovtsev with your mining accounts? Why is that a problem?''

"The poor man could not explain anything. He stood and cried like a baby. There had been a misunderstanding, he sobbed, he had always trusted engineer Pavlovtsev."

"I cannot imagine what went through his mind while he lay buried in that coffin, suffocating between leaking corpses. I could not imagine it then and I cannot now. Back then, in that sunny room, Ivanovich knew exactly what he had gained. He knew there would be no hesitation the next time he called on Chairman Golovin for a favor, whatever that favor was. And that, agent Smith, is the Kiev coffin."

"This was common knowledge?"

"You don't get it; the method is worthless without the shock. You Americans would be surprised how many men are willing to die, even that way, if allowed to prepare. The team of trusted officers that did his work was sworn to secrecy. He told them, as he told me, that if they whispered about the Kiev-coffin, they would end up in it, and he would not have them dug up. I heard him impress this on Chairman Golovin. And they were not empty words. I would never have breathed a word of this under threat of death had Ivanovich been alive."

"Did Kuznetsov know?"

"No, this was Rykov at his most private."

"So, how did Caroline Griffith?"

"He must have told her. Nobody else would."

"That is impossible."

"There is no other way. You did not know the power of this man. You can regard the Kiev coffin as a fairytale if you wish. It's a true story."

"Rykov never held a rank within the GRU or the KGB. I cannot see the power of the man."

"You won't find Rykov on organization charts. You Americans don't get it. You see that his office was advisory to the general secretary, but he was untouchable. His recommendation was always heeded. Nobody in the Soviet Union entered the nomenclature without the secret blessing of his office. More importantly, one word from him removed people from the list. Out of a quarter million in the top political and business administration, a few thousand at the top knew. They too were parents with children who wanted a better future. They wielded the power of state but owned nothing of their own. Everything they had, apartments, datjas, Zil limousines and chauffeurs, gardeners and cooks, all state property. All could be removed with a stroke of his pen. It didn't matter how high and mighty they were. If your security clearance was revoked, your family went down. That was the power of Aleksei Ivanovich."

"Caroline could not know any of this."

"That woman, agent Smith, has his genes. I knew the look in her eyes. I was a prisoner in the gulag. She said it, the zek-sense kept me alive. In my mind, this woman and Rykov are one and the same. If you think back, she called it "MY KIEV COFFIN". Nobody knew. You said you loved that piece of trash. You should have shot her there and then. Keep one thing in mind, if you ever meet her again, and if you want to live. Don't ask her about her Kiev coffin."

They studied each other in silence for too long.

"We had a deal, agent Smith. Is my answer to your satisfaction?"

"Sure, your new American friends are waiting downstairs."

CHAPTER 18

THE ANACOSTIA ASYLUM for the Criminally Insane looked like an unstaffed warehouse. She stood in the shadows on the far side of the street, keeping away from the cameras. This was not a good neighborhood.

Watching the illuminated entrance, the golden green expanse of armored glass glittered in her eyes. There was no turning back. Not with her daughter in there. Trusting her safety to agent Smith and his amateurs could only be negligent although the thought was hard to purge. He had offered his own life rather than take hers. Love was a weakness threatening to split her again. There was great strength in love. She shook her head slowly as she walked in the shadows, turning into the next street to the left of the large concrete building.

Behind a row of heavy hydraulic traffic Bollards that now protruded up through the asphalt, there was a basement garage with a metal door. On the concrete wall to the side of the door there sat a small well-lit metal door monitored by two hidden cameras. Imbedded in concrete next to the door was a card operated lock.

Off in the rubble strewn darkness, a distant argument heated up between a man and a woman. The well-rehearsed words carried in the dead of night. A door slammed. The argument faded but did not falter. This part of Anacostia was no place for a woman, but

Caroline felt no fright. The scary part was already locked up within her.

Watching for movement, she stepped quickly across the sloping court down towards the small basement door, into the light. Pushing the plastic card into the slot, she tried not to think. She punched in the code tersely, ready to bolt. She had no way of knowing whether Kuznetsov had changed the codes, but why should he with Rykov and his memory terminated.

A green light came on. Holding the Burberry carrier bag against her stomach, facing hidden cameras, she pulled open the heavy door. The hallway was empty. Relaxing, she bent to stash the wrapped plastic bag against the outside wall. It looked at home among the drifting litter, but a bag with a heavy Sig Sauer would be going nowhere. Caroline entered the hallway, and the heavy steel door slammed behind her.

Inside the main entrance, a male psychiatrist in charge of admittance studied the woman on the monitors. The Millivision camera read her body heat and registered a gun that she had decided to hide outside. He watched her enter the short passage and waited for her to enter his field of vision through the single door at the other end.

The passage had no camera. She would exit into an area used to park and process incoming ambulances. The door remained closed, but a light signaled that the woman had entered the hidden entrance in the passage, using the correct code. The Russian admittance psychiatrist felt out of his depth. He put in a call to Krivonosov, the head of Institute security to inform him of the breach; a stranger had entered the part of the basement that had no cameras. None of the staff had control over this area. The basement was strictly off-limits.

Krivonosov's call reached Vasily Kuznetsov on a scrambled phone as he relaxed after a private dinner with Dan Corwin, the NSA Deputy Director in one of the few bug-free places in Washington.

Kuznetsov stepped aside to take the call.

"Our Institute security may have been compromised, sir".

"May have?"

"A woman entered the secure area a few minutes ago. I believe it is Dr. Glyn-Griffith. She used your private codes, and the correct login. I have sealed off the basement to await your instructions. Nobody gets in or out."

It was an eerie feeling. He had inherited the codes Ivanovich used. He had not gotten around to renew them. Kuznetsov stroked his ample gray hair while he thought.

"Ivanovich was a professional. I didn't bother to change the codes. He had them in his head, nowhere else. As his head of security, so did I. Why would he give her the codes? Is she armed?"

"She left a handgun outside in a plastic bag. We picked it up, a Sig Sauer 226. Could be the gun she used in the Primacy Hotel. Our cameras detected nothing else on her body."

"I don't like this. If she is one of Rykov's, in what capacity? Was that why she accused me? I think she killed Miller. Even after killing four men, the White House is taking her party, asking about the kid. Is she looking for the child? How does she know where we keep her? None of the agencies know."

"Sergei?"

"No, the FBI agent in the Primacy taped Sergei. A friend of mine has listened to the tape. Sergei told the Glyn girl nothing."

There was a long silence. Kuznetsov smiled regretfully across the room to Dan Corwin. Sergei had told the Bureau nothing. As part of the government deal, he would be well cared for in the protection of a friendly power. He would come in handy as a conduit to the government. For some reason she had spared him. How did that woman know of his past as a political prisoner, ridiculing his zek sense? It was all too disturbing. And why taunt him with Cheka methods since the dawn of the revolution? That Kiev coffin was for historians.

"Apart from surgical equipment, I doubt she will find any weapons down there."

The basement storage area was a curiosity that he had yet to explore. Kuznetsov had been allowed down there in Rykov's company but never alone.

"Rykov did not like weapons lying around. If he had any, she won't find them."

Given her trail of surprises, he was not going to bet on it. Kuznetsov turned to make sure the NSA Deputy Director was out of earshot.

"Our official line is this; we do not know that someone has broken into the asylum basement. What we know is that there was a breach when as two of our worst psychopaths escaped down into the basement. Inform the police but explain that it is a minor internal matter of no significance. Our staff has secured the area; the patients cannot get out of there. We will find them and lock them up when we have gathered a team equipped to apprehend them."

"I will arrange it now, sir"

"Let them have the basement for a few hours before we secure it. There is no rush, and finders' keepers for the woman. Make it convincing."

"Will you be coming over, sir?"

"I need a few hours. These are delicate negotiations. Nobody knows she's there. Pick up what's left of her later. There is a grinder down there. I've seen it used. It takes whole bodies, even bones. Reward our patients for a sleepless night, give them double portions of minced meat with their pasta. Well spiced, Krivonosov. Dispose of any leftovers, and put on the screamers. Rykov was right, they are a splendid diversion. Let them sing for their supper. If the FBI comes to the asylum, or if you find the doctor alive, finish it. Let her be a victim of her illegal entry and clean up the basement. We should have her daughter ready for tomorrow. We can't afford either of them alive. We can allow the police to find the criminals who abducted her. Again, make it convincing. They can escape after killing the kid. Nothing leads back to us."

Kuznetsov put down the phone and joined his host. Dan Corwin was in good spirits and offered a Cuban cigar with the cognac. The deal was on track. The details to be ironed out were fewer by the hour. The United States Air Force had their planes in the air.

They would cross the Urals in time.

Under the circumstances, the NSA Deputy Director felt that this old semi-retired public servant should be given whatever time he needed to tend to his trivial private matters on the phone.

CHAPTER 19

IN THE NARROW hallway, Caroline heard the muted thud of well-greased deadbolts withdrawing. The low floor safety lights barely penetrated the darkness. She moved around the hallways and rooms with youthful agility. Nothing gave her fright. Not even the shelves with human parts in large glass jars. As a doctor, she had seen it all. The memories of how the parts got there were more bothersome.

For a while, she stood by the high white freezer, listening. Not a sound. She opened the freezer and its strong light split the darkness. From the top-shelf, a severed head seemed to stare after the escaping light, except it had no eyes. Part of her knew the face from a mug shot flashed at her in Georgetown Hospital. Another part knew it better, and a slow smile drew over her face.

"Orlov, old comrade, we have another night to share," she told him. "And we will have visitors."

The cold light bounced off the bright head into the operating theater and lit up a Soviet wall poster across from the dissection table. The poster glass reflected the freezer with a brilliant oblong of light that was centered by a haloed head. The slogan in Cyrillic text never failed to touch her.

YOU FOR ME AND I FOR YOU, in front of it stood a bulky meat grinder.

From somewhere in the asylum above, Caroline heard the first of the distant howls. She listened tensely until a chorus joined in. You had a strong voice, Orlov.'

She fell into a brief silence.

They had good run, she and Orlov, during the years after Beria, when the bureaucrats thought they had tamed the beast, after ousting Malenkov, especially. How he had laughed with Orlov at the twentieth Congress when the fools congratulated themselves on having the security organs under party control. They were both young then. They owned the bureaucrats who ran the union. They knew how to balance the scales, but nothing lasts forever.

"It was good to take you apart, old friend," she said.

From a hook, she picked up a sturdy leather belt, used by handy men to carry tools in. Her attempts to strap it on failed. She was too thin. This made her laugh out loud. Leaving the freezer open for the light, she walked over to the sparkling dissection table. She liked the feel of steel, draining channels, and the cutting tools. She held up a three-stranded steel pick for Orlov's indifferent gaze. It amused her how well the freezer had taught him to master a stiff upper lip.

Piercing a hole in the customized leather belt, she strapped it on and turned to rummage among the instruments, turning them over in the cold light. Satisfied, she strode into the laboratory. Vapors welled forth when she raised the lid of a large container of Dry Ice. Then suddenly light flooded the room. They had turned on the lights from upstairs. The visitors would be coming soon, three or four at the most.

She walked slowly over to the fuse box beside the freezer and threw a pair of switches. It left the basement in total darkness. The flicked a switch to enjoy the weak glow of the safety lamp by the floor. They made the game more exciting.

"Keep your cool, Orlov." She slammed the freezer shut.

Darkness leveled the playing field. Her lack of fear made her superior. The dry ice gave her an edge, as did her hiding places. With her brains and her vast knowledge of damaged human nature, she was on top of anything they could throw at her during the chase. She could display every fear that her assailants could wish for after cornering her.

"Please don't hurt me."

The hollow stammer was Caroline's rehearsal of a plea. It floated into the empty hallway. She saw herself stumbling forward, a mouse towards the cat that wounded her, slow submissive gestures seeking closure. At the same time, she recalled the thrill of sublime control, rushing through the heart of a dominant male.

Caroline paused to lend an attentive ear to distant screams, her heart cold as the dry ice.

Somewhere up there, Mary was waiting.

CHAPTER 20

J. EDGAR HOOVER called the hulking building the ugliest building he laid his eyes on. Across Pennsylvania Avenue from Justice, a thousand yards from the White House, agent Smith slammed his palm on the city map.

"She knew the Primacy would alarm Kuznetsov if she used that phone," but his carping about it did not ease the misgivings. He was talking to himself more than anyone else and his voice was thick with reproach.

"She wanted me there," he repeated. "She used me as a decoy to distract the Russians."

"She's a bag of tricks," said Parker Junior, stroking his battered nose.

"And that's not half of it. There was a phone there with a scrambler and charged batteries with her prints on it. She used it to call the desk to scare the clerk, as agent Monroe of the FBI, before her call to Kuznetsov that's supposed to be for his ears only. So, why pick the old phone that everybody taps into, including the hotel desk? How did she know that calling him this way would not only alert us but also Kuznetsov?"

"She wanted you to drop by. That's mind boggling on its own, but what about Sergei? What did she want with Sergei?"

"She set this up to get to that Russian clown. Don't make sense, Parker. She had total control. There was no fear in her. She wouldn't have spared him for a second without a reason."

"This is madness, I could have told you that," said Junior, trying to be delicate, "but Sergei told her nothing. You have it on tape."

Smith had gone deaf on him. His ragged task force was down to scraps with negative reports from all over. Caroline had vanished into thin air. Nobody had the power to put up roadblocks around the capital in a murder case, not even the president. Not even if the president had been murdered. He had agents hanging about by the hundreds, sifting through surveillance tapes, trying to spot a face. Not a single sighting from Dulles or National, or BWI. There was nothing to suggest she had left the capital. Washington Greyhound terminal, Union Station, and the Metro were covered on an outside chance, but there were too many people traveling through the larger hubs.

One of the trackers came online. Relieved of the indulgence, Smith flipped a phone speaker and sat back exhausted. His task force was all ears, hoping for a break.

"The target stopped in Anacostia, unmarked side street; seems to be a large concrete warehouse. I don't know this place. It has one main entrance of glass where he entered the building with his bodyguards. I'm going in closer."

"Kuznetsov breaks up his NSA dinner to go slumming?"

The sneer from one of the coordinators in the rom had members of Smith's task force raising their heads from less rewarding tasks. The biker came on again.

"A regular bunker, there's a name up-front. I'll read it to you; The Anacostia Asylum for the Criminally Insane."

"Kuznetsov's volunteering," somebody said.

"If you read his file, you'd know." Smith trailed off; his mind caught in a sudden flurry; the man was an accredited psychologist. It was the name that brought him to his feet.

"I know this place," said Parker Junior, ahead of him. "It's a private asylum. They handle our worst cases. It's a well-run institution. They got loads of bad characters locked up there. We use their services."

"A top-notch medical institution beyond suspicion," Smith said almost soundlessly, "Jesus, what a cover."

Junior studied him, trying to work it out.

"Any of their shrinks have strange sounding names, Junior, like Russian?"

"Sure, I met a couple," said Parker.

"Bet you have. Back home they used their profession to keep the opposition in check."

"You would be crazy to be in opposition over there anyway," said Parker, "how about sharing?"

"Play that tape for me again, the last bit."

It rolled for ten seconds. They listened to the voices. As it came to a stop, Smith repeated in a low voice.

"This is madness, they should put you away."

Smith punched the button.

"That's our friend, Sergei saving his life. They taught him old English and he speaks it fluently all through, except for one odd accent. Notice how his accent creeps up on one word. They should put *YOU* away. Gives it a whole new meaning, doesn't it?"

"You think he's pointing her to the Anacostia Asylum?"

"I'm certain of it."

"That's a load of crap, man," Parker Junior was hoping to stave off a serious misjudgment. "Why would Sergei think Caroline knew anything about the Anacostia Asylum? And what if she did, what if she knew every asylum in the country, I mean, a doctor with a photographic memory. With millions of crazies out there, why would Sergei imagine she would catch on to that specific place?"

"He's got a crazy idea she's Rykov. You know the Russians. And if Kuznetsov works there, Rykov was sure to know about it."

"Don't make this more foolish than it already is, man, they buried the X Files a long time ago."

"Damn this guy's smart. He told her without giving anything away. Only she caught it. That's why she only winged him. It was vital for Sergei to tell her without tipping off his boss. It is a natural thing to say; this is madness. Three of his men are dead on the floor. They should put YOU away, not your daughter. What a polished performance. Even Kuznetsov can't hear him pointing to the Anacostia asylum, no more than we. The hint's so vague it's almost not there."

"That's because it isn't there. We got nothing on the Anacostia asylum." Junior had a touchy edge, perhaps dwelling on the possibility of a less promising future career.

"I think she just made a move on them. That is why Kuznetsov's rushing over there, dropping the preparations for his deal."

"Your girl is a doctor socialite who wants to save her kid, as would any mother. We are not dealing with a navy seal here. To think she's going after a Russian diplomat is irrational, man."

"She's not my girl." Smith grabbed his coat, storming out, shouting out an order to one of his agents.

"Find out who owns that place and find me a judge. Get me the necessary warrants. Bring them down there. I want enough men there to carry off that building, brick by brick."

"Might be tricky," muttered Parker Junior as he caught up.

"You got that right."

"It's a concrete building."

"You are a funny guy, you know that. Think about it; nobody ever thinks about raiding an asylum. It is a perfect cover."

"Why not raid all the asylums while we are at it?" They jumped into the car with Parker at the wheel.

With his partner seething and Smith having second thoughts, they passed Justice and the National Archives, past the Trade Commission and National Galleries. Turning left on Constitution Avenue, Smith begun to regret his rashness. He should've cleared it with Moffett who was running into flak over his handling of the case. And James Wilson had landed him in this mess, after refusing to touch it. The grapevine was ripe with rumors about Jim being the dark horse out after Moffett's job.

Coming up on his right was the illuminated dome of the Capitol, watched over by a 9-foot bronze statue called Freedom. Under her skirts, dark forces were gathering clout in the halls of Congress. And now the Director wanted out, citing personal reasons. The president had asked him to stay until after the election. That's why he had threatened to fall on his sword. He could afford to be brave. As his successor, Jim would want to keep his peace with a fragmented deadlocked Congress.

Maybe he should try to reach Moffett at the Udall reception. Smith glanced left down Delaware Avenue at the arched doorways of Union Station and recalled the kids maimed by the bomb that went off under its green roof yesterday. A diversion for the Rykov hit; he guessed as much. For them it was only collateral damage. The nationwide investigation had turned up nothing.

The fresh gust of insult inflamed his loathing and lost any thought of following procedure. They passed the Supreme Court with justice on his mind and some fiery thoughts about a woman who wasn't quite his. What a lonely waste of a life. A minute later, the car crossed the river into Anacostia where justice is done according to the Bible, in the afterlife, as a reward for a lifetime of suffering.

The call came minutes before they went in, at 10:34pm. Smith was taking a last look round the concrete edifice, and Junior took the call.

The unmarked cars and vehicles commandeered from the metropolitan police packed the street, a great show of force for the impending raid. The voice from headquarters was James Wilson, head of the Washington field division.

"Yes, sir," said Parker.

"Give me special agent Carl Smith."

"Agent Smith is taking a last look around, sir."

"The order is to pull out. Immediately."

"We believe the woman's in there, sir, and her daughter."

"Somebody just called in demanding ransom for the kid. Smith is not answering his phone. Is that deliberate? Have you all gone mad? Your warrant is setting us up as a laughingstock in court."

"Right, sir, I'll tell agent Smith."

"Parker, this is a matter of national security. Agent Smith is personally involved. He is off the case. I am putting you in charge of the task force. Pull your men out now."

"He's out there, sir, with the warrant."

"Smith can find his way back. Carry out your orders, agent Parker."

Junior threw down the receiver with an incredulous sneer but the string of curses in his mind got censored by his FBI tongue. He bolted from the car to command his men. Shortly, the fleet lit up like the coming of Christmas and cars started to pull out.

"What's going on, Parker." Smith came running.

"Somebody called in a ransom demand for Mary. James Wilson ordered us to pull out, gave me the speech about national security. Put me in charge; you are too close to the case. You are sailing too close to the sun."

"I don't believe this." Smith slumped against the car. Jim was chasing the Directorship under pressure, another public contender running for cover.

"Jim got the shivers. They're working him over."

"Who?"

"I don't know. Washington power is faceless. I don't know how to deal with these guys. I can't even get past their Congress staffers. Jim's right though, this is personal."

"These are orders, man," Junior said in a disgusted voice, getting into the car, "let's go back and follow up on that ransom demand."

"They are in there. The Russian General is feeling the heat. A ransom for Mary; Caroline can't even get a loan. Everybody knows that."

"Don't mess this up, man."

"You pull out, ugly bastard. You are in charge. If you got any decency in your misshapen head, tell Jim I was already inside; I never got the message." He slammed the door and stood to watch his friend back away. The silent words shouted behind the car window were probably directing him to a warmer place.

From the broad steps, against golden green of the main entrance, he watched Parker tear off after his task force. The flashing lights melted into the darkness like a cloud of helpless fireflies.

The truth hit him under the waterline and punctured important convictions of a lifetime. He had believed the national dream. The idea had never occurred to him that he was the monkey wrench in the system, the standup guy in front of a government steamroller. It had landed him here, in No Man's Land, the one place on Earth that was exposed to attacks from both sides.

In the Anacostia darkness, he checked his gun. His Beretta did not look imposing. He entered through a wall of armored glass into a cubicle of glass and marble where another glass wall blocked his passage. The ceiling of this holding pen was fifteen feet high. Beyond it was a roomy entrance hall, no less impressive. The armored sheets of glass sunk into both the floor and the walls. No weak points.

The glass wall had a glass door set in a frame of polished steel, no handles either way. The marble wall to his right had a small sheet of armored glass inserted. Behind it, at the reception desk, sat the admission shrink in a white coat tainted green by four inches of glass. The man eyed him without commitment. He could not tell if the visitor was a professor or a patient. There was no difference until you sorted them out.

"I understand Dr. Kuznetsov has arrived." Smith spoke into a hidden microphone. "Tell him that special agent Carl Smith of the FBI is here to see him."

The man examined him in silence. Without anything to offer but empty threats, Smith knew that if the shrink chose to ignore him, he had no backing. These walls had withstood more than the gripes of an unhappy federal agent. If Caroline was half right, the men who ran this outfit knew he was here in defiance of his orders.

"Immediately, please." Smith flashed his warrant card.

In a silent world, he watched the psychiatrist make his call. Smith had a vague sense of howling coming from somewhere in the background. The sound barely made it out through the glass.

"What is this about," a loudspeaker asked.

"We have a search and seizure warrant for these premises. It is a politically sensitive matter. We do not want to use the warrant. It is better to handle the matter quietly. I represent people who need a word to secure a satisfying outcome."

There was another silent period as he watched the man on the other side mouth words. He thought of watertight compartments of marionettes and masters, twice removed. He thought of Caroline.

"Wait inside please."

The reply came as Smith heard the bolts of the steel framed glass door withdraw, and the door opened to a howling sound as he pushed through. You could not get at the reception clerk from that side either. He was shielded by another sheet of green glass. For a loony bin, these were draconian arrangements. As he looked around, an armed posse of three came to escort him up the flight of stairs to the lion's den. He was in their hands now and he didn't like it.

"We ask to surrender gun." The man in charge of this alien world was a muscular guy. "No weapons unless staff," he told the visitor. The urge was growing on Smith to collect for grievances past. The broken English, the bodybuilder types that Caroline had dispatched so practically.

"Forget it, pal," he said calmly, "I'm the law here. I'm the one with the search warrant." He had to speak loud because of the savage howling that engulfed them.

"Institution rule."

"Boris; the men who made my rules, carry a bigger stick."

They moved closer as they walked, menacing him. The familiarity pissed him off. There were three of them and he was the smallest guy around.

"It is a federal offense punishable by law to threaten a federal agent." He knew words would not bring them to heel. Elbowing one of them away, he distanced himself enough to pull his gun. Feet apart, left arm supporting the right, the Beretta aimed at the chest in charge. It was hilarious but he was so tired of this shitshow that he almost wanted to die, at least get the nonsense over with.

"You are under arrest, all three of you. You have the right to remain silent."

The Russian eyed him coldly as he plucked from his chest a digital intercom, clipped to the pocket. He spoke Russian, cupping his hand to block off the howling sound that permeated everything. He turned more cooperative, if no less arrogant.

"Mr. Smith, there has been breakout. Two of our most dangerous patients are hiding in the basement. If not surrender gun, we ask you be careful that nobody takes it away from you."

"You must be kidding."

"Dr. Aleksandrovich will see you now."

Smith felt relief as a thick door closed behind him, cutting off the screaming. The general's large study was soundproof. He supposed it had to be in his racket.

It was a cultured room. The former KGB general took his stand behind a big mahogany roll-top desk. Behind him on the wall there hung a late mythological Baroque tapestry of frolicking youths. Like other antique pieces, left and right, it served no purpose but to flaunt gravy. Smith walked across a vast Tabriz carpet in blue, brick red and ivory. A heavy ornamental leather sofa was more authentically Russian than its owner but overstuffed to match his Ukrainian ego.

They were alone. Kuznetsov did not like the intrusion, but he was a careful sort and curious. Had he missed an ingredient in his brinkmanship? Smith knew he must her him out. The man didn't offer him a seat but stood waiting, his voice and manner condescending.

"You are here in conflict with your standing orders, agent Smith. James Wilson, your superior, assured me of this a moment ago. I reached him through a mutual friend, Reisman, Director of the National Security Agency. Wilson agreed with Reisman that you were up the wall on probable cause; those were his words."

"Let's say, I represent other interests," Smith lied as smoothly as he knew how.

"I see."

The former general was a brilliant bureaucrat with a sharp mind, schooled in staying on top. Kuznetsov watched him intently and his benign smile started to grate on Smith. The man gave nothing away.

"How can I help, agent Smith?"

"Dr. Caroline Glyn-Griffith identified you as the assassin Aleksei Ivanovich Rykov, the majority owner of this institution."

"A misunderstanding; I was dining with Dan Corwin, deputy director of the National Security Agency when that incident took place, and I don't know her motive for telling his tale. There is an agreement between the United States and Russia hanging in the balance. A new era of security is at stake. Unfortunately, there are people in both our nations who don't want this deal to go through. Why would I murder my most trusted friend?"

"Acting for general Orlov?"

Faced with no response, he changed tact.

"I have reason to believe that Dr Glyn-Griffith may think you are holding her daughter within these walls."

"This is intolerable, agent Smith. Your superior James Wilson told me a minute ago that the Bureau has a new lead in the kidnapping of her daughter."

"General, given the mothers state of mind, we have reason to believe that she may try to break into this building. I doubt that she will find it an easy task, but Caroline has a remarkable ability to surprise. If she tries to enter this institution illegally, I want your commitment to hand her over to the authorities in good physical health."

They watched each other in silence for a while. The former general neither confirmed nor denied the possibility. In his book, it was the way to avoid traps. Smith pushed on.

"Yesterday I had a long meeting with Alexander Downey, the president's Chief of Staff. Although we agree there is greater good hanging in the balance, it is essential that the media does not get whiff of more bloodshed." Smith made a point of a small hesitation. "These vulgar incidents must stop. They are becoming a political embarrassment."

"Running errands for the White House?"

Smith shrugged and remained silent. So far, he had not lied. The rare old animal would understand. You might count on powerful alliances for protection but you never knew if they were virtual or real. With alarm he watched the stoic bureaucrat dial, slowly and with infinite patience. Smith had not counted on the phone.

"General Vasily Aleksandrovich Kuznetsov for Alexander Downey," the Ukrainian watched him as he spoke. Smith was careful not to bat an eyelid.

"Alexander, I call to thank you personally for your invitation, the private lunch tomorrow. It is most kind."

"Looking forward to it," boomed a familiar voice through the loudspeaker. The Ukrainian fox was playing it openly.

"One other matter; I spoke to a young man today, name of Smith. I doubt if you have heard of this FBI agent. He mentioned your name on bringing me some advice. Would you be willing to vouch for this young man?"

"Agent Carl Smith gave us the key to go forward with your deal. He raised several points of common interests. Listen to the man."

The chief of staff, hiding behind his cheerful campaign voice, might be hamstrung by lack of information but he knew where his loyalties lay. Smith was grateful for that.

"Splendid, Alexander, tomorrow then."

The general replaced the phone, smiling.

"Political embarrassment; what a strange argument to use. Are you not aware that political embarrassment is the lifeblood of your government?"

Kuznetsov beckoned the lowly agent to a modern Barcelona Chair by Van Der Rohe, a fact that slipped Smith's mind. The older man started to stop tobacco into a Dunhill pipe with a crooked stem that suited its owner. Smith watched him commence to light this contraption with a long wooden match. It was clearly a long dear affectation.

"Without embarrassment," the general continued and flicked a hand to put out the match, "there is no progress. In our great Sovietzni Soyuza we did not have political embarrassment for half a century."

He pulled on his pipe with a satisfied look and leaned back in the high-backed official chair, received by creaking leather.

"You know where that got us."

"Are you holding Mary, her daughter?"

"Of course not, that is delusional. I cannot imagine where this personal hatred comes from, but I suspect that Aleksei Ivanovich had a hand in it."

"Your most trusted friend," asked Smith.

"The Anacostia Asylum for the Criminally Insane is a noble institution. Would we endanger its reputation for such nonsense?"

"That will please the new majority owner."

"What new majority owner?" The surprise was genuine.

"Whoever inherits Rykov, surely," said Smith.

There had been no leaks from the White House strategy planning session. He had the general at a disadvantage but could not really press the point.

"Has there to your knowledge been any attempt made to enter the building, illegally or not?"

"This is a bad neighborhood. We have attempted break-ins almost every night. I hear that someone entered our basement area earlier tonight, using secret codes to our electric locks. We have no evidence that this is your friend. We have no pictures from the back entrance, and we cannot explain how the intruder got hold of the codes, unless whoever had worked closely with Ivanovich."

"Where is she now?" The alarm shot through him.

"As I said, we do not who the intruder is. As far as we know, he is still in the basement. We haven't been able to search it. You are aware that we had a breakout of two criminally active patients earlier tonight. We reported this matter to the police. They escaped into the basement laboratories. It is a minor problem, aside from the risk they might kill each other. We have sealed off all the exits to the basement to contain them. At the time, we had no knowledge of anyone else being down there."

"Caroline is down there with these animals?"

His voice betrayed emotional involvement, and this was not lost on the general. Hiding was no longer important. Kuznetsov had trapped her in the cellar and set his animals on her. This lowlife would also get away with it, for the good of the nation.

"Believe me, young man. If the intruder is your young ward, there is no hope for her. In that case I am sorry for your loss. Many hours went by before our staff realized the breach. I returned here as soon as I heard.

The psychopaths down there find raping their victims, male or female less than satisfying. They like to mutilate, sometimes eat them, preferably alive." The old man shook his head ruefully over such excesses.

"You haven't seen Caroline in action."

"If we though there was a chance to find the intruder alive, we would have gone down there half an hour ago. At this point, you are delaying me. The team is waiting on my orders. We do know that both our patients are alive."

"How do you know that?"

The general took a moment to puff the pipe alive, a thin benign smile passing his lips. "We can track them. All our patients wear a metal armband they cannot get rid of. They are still in the basement. The bracelet has a temperature detector. If body temperature drops below 95 degrees Fahrenheit, a person is dead. Both our patients are still alive."

"And you're just sitting there. Have you heard anything?"

"You mean like screaming? As you heard in the hallway, any screams from down there would be hard to sort out." The general relaxed in his chair and nurtured the pipe.

"Our team is ready to go down there to locate and bring back our two patients. We have delayed this long enough. If you want to go down there with them to corroborate our procedures, I will not stand in your way, but you must follow their rules."

Kuznetsov reached for a button on his desk. A moment later a man entered the office in a heavy protective gear with a custom-made riot helmet. Entering with him was the howling.

"We are ready, sir."

Kuznetsov moved his redwood Dunhill to his right and rose from the creaking leather. He looked at Smith.

"Our four-man retrieval team can flush them out. They will do this systematically. They will seek out the burglar or whatever remains of him or her. The basement is a big place, and this is dangerous work. We have proven methods to deal with them. They are mental patients, not criminals. If you use your gun on our patients, we will press charges. You are free to go with them as an observer, but we cannot guarantee your safety."

Smith strode out into the white hallway without a word. The sharp rise in sound level hit him like a brick. Had they set these guys screaming to hide the fate of his woman? He did not put it past them.

Three heavily protected men waited in the hallway outside the office with taut faces. They carried loads of equipment but no smiles. To them the excursion was no joke. The animals in the basement were real.

Smith couldn't hear Kuznetsov's orders to the team leader. If he had, they would not have surprised him.

"If her death looks natural, let him live to bear witness. If there is anything that can't stand public inquiry, agent Smith must be dealt with."

Kuznetsov chose his words carefully. The armored man waited. He was in no hurry to go into that basement.

"If you must deal with agent Smith, do it in a way that is not, how can I put this; politically embarrassing."

CHAPTER 21

ISOLATED WATER PIPES and electrical cables lined the top of the roughcast walls. In the dark, along endless whitewashed corridors, they found many of the doors to be locked and sealed. Mostly, the retrieval team shone their flashlights through the dusk to check for broken seals. Then they passed on, leaving Smith to wonder what the asylum hid within these rooms, presumably medical records. It was a great place to keep records where the Department of Justice couldn't have a look. Occasional safety lights by the floor helped them negotiate the endless corridors, their points of dusk alternating with darkness.

The floor had vinyl coating that squeaked under the synthetic soles that Smith wore for friction. Suddenly the vinyl started to feel sticky under his shoes and someone bellowed "Skolzko!" Then the floor turned slippery. The distant howls unnerved Smith more than he cared to admit. The dark red flecks in the beam of his borrowed flashlight explained the tension.

There was blood on the walls too.

Smith clamped a lid on his private thoughts. He didn't want to speculate what these criminals had done to Caroline. He tried to focus on retribution. Without access, retribution was a pipe dream.

With the pressures brought to bear by the Iron Triangle and the vast sums of money involved, political lives were on the line and political fallout spread like expanding rings on water. In the West Wing of the White House, he had met the high priests. Behind them in shadows of anonymity, a mighty army of powerful bureaucrats wielded enormous influence.

A heart stuffed with raw hatred or shot through with rage was no help when you were left out of the loop. Besides, he could never be sure if Caroline had chosen to throw him back into the pond. The small catch.

There were vapors of dry ice in the air as the five of them advanced ponderously through the darkened hallways. The four-member retrieval team moved ahead of Smith in a tight round group. They walked back-to-back in a way that allowed four sets of eyes to scan all directions. Smith couldn't tell them apart. They wore a cumbersome outfit. Back-to-back, they formed interchangeable parts of an eight-legged armored spider.

As the odd man out, Smith followed, left to tend his own safety, was well aware that he was the bait that would draw the bigger catch. Coming down to the wire, he was no longer tired enough to die.

Walking behind the eight-legged spider with strung nerves, the Beretta felt snug in his hand. The others packed nothing heavier than tranquilizers and stun guns. Their strength lay in numbers and training. They had body armor to protect them, and expensive night vision goggles and batons. Their task was to subdue two unarmed mental patients, and a professional handling was essential, playing this charade for posterity.

The brutal murder of Dr. Caroline Glyn-Griffith, now about to be revealed, would demand a full enquiry. In the murky waters of beltway politics, that investigation would be lax enough to sink without trace. It would be buried behind the blue wall of silence.

The armored eight-legged spider jerked to an abrupt stop as orders were exchanged over the open radio link in four helmets. The ceiling was lower here. The spider spotted a shape up-front. Vapors of dry ice played hide-and-seek. The spider inched closer. A form emerged out of the dark. A body hung from a hook in the ceiling, much of it missing. The black spider remained still, patiently watching all four directions, sensing a trap. Smith raced ahead without a thought for safety. He couldn't tell if it was Caroline, or what was left of her. There was no head, no genitals.

The spider edged closer, two sets of eyes watching the agent pull at a shredded blood-soaked shirt, the other two pair of eyes watching the spiders back.

For a second, he lost heart, as the carcass swung on its roped hook. Spotting a tattoo, Smith exhaled, and inhaled deeply of the dry ice fumes.

The built-in two-way radio crackled in Russian. Smith, who had only a rudimentary understanding of the language, fought to catch the garbled message.

"General. We found Timmons dead, with his arm missing. Somebody is wearing his armband, probably Mercer."

Somewhere off in the vaporous semidarkness, an old bulky machine broke through the distant screams as it started to growl.

"Somebody switched on the meat grinder, general."

"Check it out."

Again, they were moving carefully down a hallway with Smith trailing behind.

"Ostorozno stupen," barked the leading head. Mind your step, Smith decided.

Two steps down, they entered an operating theater. The spider moved cautiously towards the source of a metallic sound. It eased to a halt when it came upon a steel container overflowing with minced meat. The growling was forceful enough to give the upstairs screamers a run for it.

"Is it the woman?" crackled the general from the comfort of his upstairs study. The black spider studied the steel drum.

"How the hell would I know?"

The snarled words threw up a whisk of insubordination. It was a sight to kill anybody's appetite. The general had asked if it was the woman. There could be no doubt that the gender of their illicit intruder had been known from the start.

In the center of the unlit room, the spider spun slowly. The vapors were denser. Four sets of eyes took in a stunned special agent who stood frozen with a Beretta and a borrowed flashlight. He was looking into a softly lit microwave oven. It caught the spider's attention. Again, the radio crackled as the team moved closer to the source of light. The sparkling green number 95 was displayed in the digital window. Body temperature! Two hands were visible through the glass, severed above the wrist. Both wore metal bracelets.

"Timmons and Mercer are dead, general. The woman's alive."

Strangely, it soothed the frightened spider, if not the general. Smith was thrilled but confused.

As the tension fell away, the spider came apart. The four men had feared the enemy they knew. They moved swiftly to secure the empty room and adjoining hallway. A woman was easily dealt with. That attitude was tested when the spider came apart, and one of them found three heads in the freezer.

"We found their heads in the freezer, sir. We also found the head of general Orlov. How can we explain that to the agent?"

"Find the Doktorom and kill her," ordered the armchair general, "and the Amerikanskij, use a knife." A scream from the hallway cut his command short.

"Where's Pankin?" crackled out of the radio of two helmets. They all spun around to check on each other, looking to find the one fourth that was missing, lost out in the hallway vapors.

"Pankin!" the leader called out, releasing his plastic visor. There was no answer.

With disturbing speed, a newborn three-sided spider moved off briskly, its six feet slipping and skidding in the hallway. The team ignored Smith. He was no threat to them. The hunt was not over. It had just begun. Three pair of eyes found the floor covered with fluid, and intestines. True to its nature, the spider followed a string of gut to a black and red figure wobbling on the vinyl floor, its armor flayed open, half the insides of an open stomach gone. The man babbled in shock.

"Pankin's down!" the spider crackled as it came apart, all eyes on the small red footprints that disappeared into the vapors. They pulled knives from under their armor.

In the wild chase that ensued, Smith released the safety and backed off, only to slip on a piece of gut. Coming down hard, he crawled away on all four, lost in an unknown labyrinth, and he hated spiders more than ever. He knew that professionalism was no longer essential. Their patients were dead. He was not the prime target, but they'd kill anything that moved.

Somewhere up ahead, the unknown enemy must have caught up with the rest of the spider because a roar of pain echoed through the hallways, then a thrashing sound as another shout broke into a moan.

Smith rose and stepped carefully forward, stumbling over a body. He bent to shine his flashlight at a steel handle of a long instrument, protruding downwards from between a helmet, stabbed upwards into the man's skull from the side of the neck. Could this be the work of Caroline, his Caroline?

He ventured closer to the unrestrained voices of the remaining hunters, unwilling to use his flashlight to draw attention. There was a struggle going on. He moved quickly, in haste born of fear, this time not for his benefit.

In front of Smith, among the dancing shadows, someone cursed in Russian. He could make out a big dark figure thrashing a smaller one against the wall. Stepping closer, he shifted the flashlight in his left to allow the wrist to support his right hand, holding both the gun and beam on the same target.

The small intruder had wounded one of them, a bulky figure crawling away on the floor, while the biggest part of the spider had moved in to gain the advantage. Both seemed to be bleeding. The dazed woman seemed no longer to care. The spent creature did not look anything like Caroline, drenched in blood and madness.

Smith kept a more leisurely image of this woman, resting naked by his side against pink pajamas. This was someone else, or was it? Her lack of weight tired her as they struggled. The armored man had lost his knife on the floor, but his power was overwhelming.

Pinned down, she didn't have the strength. The man pounded the thin figure against the wall in a burst of rage and the woman went momentarily still. A sleek steel tool slipped from her hand. The man bent to pick it up, holding the long steel blade low, setting her up for the kill.

His orders were clear.

Smith pulled the trigger calmly once, watching in cold horror as the slug entered from the side through the base of his neck, the weakest point of his protective armor. The man fell from her. This was not by the book. He had given no warning.

Coming out of it, the bloody creature shot him a lightning look with a knitted brow, focusing against the beamed light. Smith let his arm drop and saw a mild faraway smile come over her trancelike face. Then, with a sudden start, she melted away.

Caroline had remembered Mary.

Smith started to run, trying to place her footfalls in the dark, groping through the vapors. He could not afford to lose her again.

He was shouting her name when he suddenly came upon the broad stairway to the basement. The open door above confirmed that she was going for the impossible.

Caroline felt as if she had entered up from the underworld. With her roughed up face and caked hair, her ripped and blood-soaked clothes, all bathed in light, she was out of place in clean white corridors.

A deadly quiet had descended. The screamers had fallen silent. She walked swiftly towards the soundproof office door. Her mind was hard and clear, and her bare feet left footsteps on the floor, bloody like a soviet banner. She didn't know where they kept Mary but there was a deal in the making; a deal for the well-being of Vasily Aleksandrovich Kuznetsov.

Her drive for that deal fell apart as she entered.

Kuznetsov was a shrewd psychologist. Even so, he would not have expected the love for a child to become Rykov's undoing twice. In his mind he had already dispatched that old monster.

Kuznetsov had fetched Mary.

Caroline took one look at her daughter and her heart broke. She saw a pale raven-haired child, alone and forlorn on an overstuffed leather sofa at her wit's end, after listening to the screamers.

Mary looked up at her in the doorway as fear took over her daughter's face. She did not recognize her mother. There was no joy in this reunion. How could she dream that this blood caked ogre, this pulped up and sliced visitor from hell, was her loving mother?

Caroline lost it.

All the cold and clever resolutions were swept aside in a tidal wave of gratified emotions. Her mind broke, and confusion set in. She run across the Tabriz carpet to embrace a terrified girl who tried to pull away. She had run like that towards her daughter once before, on that Georgetown Street. It had killed the other half of her.

Now she tried to speak to her daughter in a normal voice to make her understand that Mom had come to save her. But she had lost it.

There was no longer any place for the stranger within. Like a thin veil of frost, Rykov's icy mind had melted away in the furnace of her love, and Caroline had exorcised the demon.

Kuznetsov sat at his desk, drawing on his crooked pipe. He wore white cotton gloves as he picked up the Sig Sauer she had left at the back entrance. He watched with detached interest as the woman spoke rapidly to calm the crying child. It was all coming apart.

The call from Dan Rayburn moments earlier was deeply worrying. Senator Greenbaum, of all people, had accused the two of them of defrauding the United States Air Force. He could not work out why the authorities were turning against him? Timothy Udall who chaired research and development on the House Armed Services Committee was not a man to be easily brushed aside.

In this game of fox and geese, the hounds had him cornered. The uranium deal would be cleared but with his subsequent reputation at risk, he needed firm answers. With the eyes of the agencies on him, waiting for the truth was not a luxury he could afford. The Sig was hers. He must bring her to the basement where he had enough bodies to make a case. The child would be escorted away from here to disappear without a trace. He must leave the country until another national emergency called for a new deal in the national interest.

Kuznetsov raised the heavy gun.

Out of touch, Caroline was embracing Mary when the shot rang out. The general toppled off his armchair, sparks flying from his pipe. His abrupt departure left the chair slowly spinning, much like the downstairs spider.

Caroline looked at the man in the doorway, bigger than he had any right to be. Wired for action, Smith thought she came back to reality with that troubled smile. Badly sliced halfway down to her elbow, her shoulder looked bad, the skin parting with the blood-soaked sleeve. And still she smiled. She was back with the people she loved. He could not know that she had washed away that evil presence.

Seconds later, Smith walked mother and child down the airy hall towards the main exit. They passed by an office with several staff members that seemed unwilling to intervene. He suspected that the medical staff had turned a blind eye to the evils of this place as a payback for a corrupt past. How loyal would they be with the general and his thugs gone? Smith released the safety on his gun.

From what he had seen, the fear of reprisal weighed heavier than the privilege of working for good money in a free country. There would be no help to be had from these people. Smith realized he had no way to get the girls out through the heavily bolted door in the reinforced glass wall.

The sound came at them like an explosion. The gun slipped in the sweat of his palm as the shock went through the concrete bunker. He tightened his grip to steady the gun as he pulled them back from a cacophony of crashing glass. He had slammed Caroline against the wall, trying not to hurt the child in her arms.

Smith eased forward to look down into the glass and marble entrance.

"What happened?" Caroline winced at the pain from her open skin as Mary buried her head in her shoulder, crying.

"We have a visitor," said Smith.

The wall of glass had come crashing down over the front of a colossal earthmover. The giant machine had penetrated half its size into the roomy entrance hall.

Through the clearing dust, a big man threads his catlike way in among cracked slabs of glass, a black ugly bastard who spent a football scholarship learning how to run into other people at high speed. He was asking the stunned admittance psychiatrist beyond the green reception glass if he was coming out, or if he was coming in.

William Parker Junior had returned with his task force.

"Who is it," asked Caroline.

"The most beautiful man you ever saw," he said.

CHAPTER 22

I T WAS EARLY Sunday morning, coming down. Caroline sneaked a look in the hall mirror. She always felt the same flood of relief when the face in the mirror was her own. It was two weeks now and she was firmly back to normal. Sanity was a short man in her bed. Caroline was happy.

It was a beautiful morning. The three of them took a walk in Fort Reno Park. Mary's knee was working up, so they walked slowly. Caroline reached out to discretely massage Carl's buttock where she plunged that pin. It was not an easy gesture; Caroline was taller, and her arm was still tightly bandaged.

Mary held on to Babushka. It was a fine moment.

Smith broke from them to throw the ice-cream wrappers in a public dustbin. He stopped to give mother and child a wistful look as they walked away, silhouetted against the sun-drenched mist of the park, a splendid blonde and her raven-haired child on a Sunday morning walk.

Nothing would ever top this. Could it possibly last?

Smith had not told Caroline about Rykov's will. Figured she would hear about it soon enough. He was also bound by an oath not to reveal it. Moffett had been clear on that.

Would it please Caroline that she would soon be the sole owner of the insurance company that battled her in court over her husband's brain tumor? He doubted it. She had no memory of her own brutal actions. She needed all the rest she could get.

Smith smiled at a private thought from last night. His woman was nothing if not kinky, and yet she looked ravishing and innocent.

He watched Caroline walk away, leading her daughter by the arm with an awkward grip so high above the wrist that Mary had to walk lopsided. It was a strange way to lead a child.

Agent Smith made a playful start and ran after them.

THE END